TRAPPED
IN A VIDEO GAME

THE INVISIBLE
INVASION

Dustin Brady

Illustrations by Jesse Brady

Andrews McMeel
PUBLISHING®

Andrews McMeel Publishing
a division of Andrews McMeel Universal
1130 Walnut Street, Kansas City, Missouri 64106

www.andrewsmcmeel.com

18 19 20 21 22 SDB 10 9 8 7 6 5 4 3 2 1

ISBN: 978-1-4494-9617-3

Library of Congress Control Number: 2018932210

Made by:
Shenzhen Donnelley Printing Company Ltd.
Address and location of manufacturer:
No. 47, Wuhe Nan Road, Bantian Ind. Zone,
Shenzhen China, 518129
1st Printing—4/23/18

Acknowledgments

Special thanks to Jesse Brady for the cover and interior illustrations. You can check out more of Jesse's sweet artwork at jessebradyart.com.

Other Books by Dustin Brady

Trapped in a Video Game

Superhero for a Day: The Magic Magic Eight Ball

Who Stole Mr. T?: Leila and Nugget Mystery #1

The Case with No Clues: Leila and Nugget Mystery #2

Bark at the Park: Leila and Nugget Mystery #3

Contents

CHAPTER 1

The Ghost

What did you do last night? Sleep? Hmm, you don't say.

Want to know what I did? I talked to an army guy. Not like someone from the real army trying to recruit me (I'm 12. It would have been a short conversation). The army guy I talked to happened to be six inches tall and made of plastic.

I don't make a habit of talking to toys—I'm not crazy—but I had a good excuse. This one talked to me first. See, I met this particular toy when he wasn't a toy but a real sergeant in the game *Full Blast*. Two weeks ago, I got sucked into *Full Blast* with my friend Eric Conrad. We flew around with jet packs and rode the Statue of Liberty like a rocket ship and almost got trapped inside the game for good by an alien who said our names in the creepiest way possible. It's a long story. You should read it sometime.

Anyways, in *Full Blast*, we met Mark Whitman—another kid from our class who had gotten sucked into the same game. Mark stayed behind so Eric and I could escape. Now, this army guy was telling me that I could go back into the video game to save Mark, but I had to "go back now."

Of course I wanted to go back. I'd do anything for Mark. The sergeant asked me if I was sure. Yes, I was sure—let's go! I stared at the army guy, waiting for him to—I don't know, click his heels or open a portal in my closet or something. Instead, he stared at me motionless, kind of like a toy would. That's when I started feeling stupid.

"Hey, I said 'yes.'" I poked the sergeant. He continued staring with his blank toy expression. "Do I need to press some sort of button?" I picked him up and turned him over in my hand. No button.

At this point, you might be thinking that maybe the whole talking toy thing was a dream. And I would normally agree with you, except for one very important detail: The sergeant had actually woken me up from a dream. Now have you ever woken up from a dream only to find yourself in another dream? You have not. That has never once happened in real life—only in movies. The talking sergeant was not a dream because this is not a movie, and also I am not crazy.

I spent the next several minutes talking to and poking at the army guy. Then I got up and checked all the places where he might have hidden some sort of portal to the video game (TV, toilet, wardrobe, etc.). Nothing. I crawled back into bed and spent much of the rest of the night convincing myself I wasn't crazy, and then I think I fell asleep.

"Jesse! Breakfast!"

My eyes popped open. Sunlight streamed through the window. Monday morning.

"Jesse!" my mom yelled up the stairs again.

"Mmmf," I replied. I stumbled out of bed and *plop-plop-plopped* down the stairs. I took my seat at the table and waited for my dad to grab the cereal from the top shelf. "What kind do you want, hon?" he asked.

"Blueberry crunch," my mom replied as she finished packing her lunch.

"I'll try that new chocolate one," I said.

My dad grabbed the blueberry only. "Can I try the chocolate one?" I repeated a little louder. My dad set my mom's cereal box on the table and grabbed his bowl from the freezer. ("Freeze the bowl first. It will change your life," he tells everyone who will listen. Not true.

From personal experience, I can tell you that the only thing freezing the cereal bowl will do is turn the milk so cold that it hurts your teeth.)

I sighed and reached for my mom's gross organic blueberry cereal. I knew the promise of chocolate for breakfast was too good to be true.

"Did you call Jesse?" my dad asked as he grabbed the cereal box before I could.

I squinted at him and waved right in front of his face. "Yeah, Dad, I'm right here."

My mom sighed. "I'll call him again." She walked to the stairs. "Jesse! Jesse Daniel Rigsby! Get down here now! You're going to be late for school!"

I threw my hands into the air. "Dad. Dad! DAD!"

My dad finished pouring his cereal and reached across the table for the milk like I wasn't there. I jumped up and grabbed the milk before he could to get his attention. That didn't stop him, so I pulled the milk toward me. Or at least I tried to pull it toward me. When I did, my hands went *right through* the jug.

"WHAT IS GOING ON?!" I grabbed the cereal box. Same thing—I could touch and feel the box, but when I tried to move it, my hand went right through.

"AHHHHH!" I ran to the bathroom and looked in the mirror, desperate to see my terrified face. Instead, all I got was the empty bathtub behind me. I looked down at my hands. Real as could be. But when I waved them in front of the mirror—nothing.

I was a ghost.

And that wasn't even the worst of it. As I tried to figure out what to do next (What do ghosts eat? Do they go to the bathroom? What about school? Is there a special ghost school?), I heard a snort behind me. I looked into the mirror. Nothing. Another snort.

I slowly turned around. Behind me, sitting patiently in the tub as real as could be, was an eight-foot-tall, bright-blue Bigfoot.

CHAPTER 2

Aug-whatever Reality

I ran out of the bathroom as fast as my little ghost legs would take me. As I passed through the kitchen, I screamed a warning to my parents. "MONSTER! MONSTER IN THE BATHROOM! DON'T GO IN!" My mom continued packing her lunch, and my dad continued eating his freezing-cold cereal as if there weren't a GIANT BLUE MONSTER IN THEIR BATHTUB!

If I didn't get some fresh air soon, I was going to pass out. I ran for the front door, grabbed the knob, twisted, and, of course, nothing happened because I was twisting with my invisible ghost hand. I took a deep breath, lowered my shoulder, and pushed into the door. There was a moment of resistance before— *pop!*—I stumbled right through solid oak.

Outside looked like a scene from *Monsters, Inc.* A herd of giant purple Ninja Turtle things strolled past my house. A fluffy, polka-dotted bird poked its head out of the tree on our front lawn and squawked. I looked down to see a pile of fur the size of a soccer ball checking out my shoelaces. When I moved my foot, it tripped over itself trying to run away.

I started breathing faster. This is not OK. THIS IS NOT OK!

"Psst."

I looked around. That "psst" sounded a lot more human than monster.

"Psst," the voice whispered again. "Jesse. Bushes."

I looked at the bushes next to the porch and noticed a cell phone pointed at me. I squinted and lowered my head. There was a guy in there. I kicked away the ball of fur that had regained the courage to battle my shoelaces again and approached the bush.

As I walked closer, I noticed the crazy hair. "Mr. Gregory?"

Mr. Gregory is the dad of Charlie Gregory, one of the kids in my class, and he works at Bionosoft, the video game company that made *Full Blast*. He promised to help me and Eric find Mark and then disappeared two weeks ago. At that moment, he was curled up in the

azalea bush, which is something that would get him in pretty big trouble if my mom saw.

"Hi," he whispered, still pointing the phone at me. "You OK?"

"I'm invisible," I hissed. "So no, I am not OK!"

"You don't have to whisper," he said. "No one can hear you."

"No kidding." I kicked the ball of fur away again. "Wait, you can hear me though, right?"

"Those things have really sharp teeth and a lot of angry friends," Mr. Gregory said. "I wouldn't make him mad."

I stopped kicking.

"But right," he continued. "Of course I can hear you. Anyone playing the game can hear you."

"What game?"

Mr. Gregory looked at me like I was crazy. *"Go Wild."*

"Okayyyyy."

He continued with the weird look. "You knew you were in *Go Wild*, right? I thought the sergeant was pretty clear."

"Pretend I have no idea what *Go Wild* even is."

"You serious?"

"I don't play video games."

"I mean, most people who enjoy *Go Wild* don't usually play video games. The core market includes . . ."

"Can you just tell me what it is?"

"Oh right, well, it's augmented reality," he said like "aug-whatever reality" is a thing people say all the time.

"Listen," I said. "I am having a real hard time right now understanding why I'm a ghost in a world of monsters, so it would be helpful if you could explain things to me in a way that a sixth-grader who is pretty new to the whole ghost thing can understand."

"First of all, you're not a ghost because you're not dead," Mr. Gregory said.

"Well, that's a relief."

"You're just in a video game. This one is like *Pokémon Go*. Do you know *Pokémon Go*?"

"I've heard of it."

"It's a game that's going on all the time in the real world. You just can't see it unless you're looking at the world through your phone. See, look."

I bent down and looked at his phone, which was pointed at my neighbor's rosebushes. On the screen, I could see the bushes as if the phone were in camera mode.

"I don't know what I'm supposed to be looking at," I said.

He tapped his phone a few times until a big cartoon pear appeared on the screen. Then he flicked his finger, which threw the pear toward the rosebushes. I looked up just in time to see the pear fly through the air and land right next to the bushes in real life.

"Whoa, how did you do that?!"

"That pear is part of the game. It's not real. Nobody can see it unless they're looking at it through their phone."

"Or unless they're in the game," I said.

"Right."

Just then a skinny snake with a gigantic head and goofy eyes emerged from the rosebushes. It examined the pear.

I jumped back. "Whoa!"

"Again, that's invisible to anyone who's not looking at it through the game on their phone," Mr. Gregory said. "Watch this."

He tapped and swiped a few more times on his screen. All of a sudden, a purple gecko thing with a long neck popped out of his phone. In a matter of two seconds, it grew a REALLY long neck to half the size of my house. It locked eyes with the snake and got angry.

"You might want to take a step back," Mr. Gregory said.

I took five steps back.

The gecko screeched. The snake hissed. The sun dimmed, and intense battle music started playing out of nowhere. The snake's eyes began glowing red. After three seconds of brighter and brighter glowing, the eyes shot two fireballs toward the gecko. As the fireballs were in midair, the gecko turned from purple to red. It absorbed the blast into its red body and grew twice as big. It then grabbed the snake by the tail, threw it into its mouth, and swallowed it in one gulp. With that, the gecko disappeared back into Mr. Gregory's phone, the lights came back on, and the music stopped.

Mr. Gregory turned to me. "You can't let that happen to you."

"I WOULD LIKE VERY MUCH FOR THAT NOT TO HAPPEN TO ME!" I yelped.

"The goal of the game, since apparently you've never played it before," Mr. Gregory gave me a skeptical look, "is to capture Wild Things. You do this by battling the Wild Things you find in the wild with Wild Things that you've already captured from the wild."

"You said 'wild' five times in two seconds."

"So when I saw that Cobrameano in the wild . . ."

"Six. Also, I don't know what that is."

" . . .When I saw that snake, I could capture it into my phone by defeating it with one of my own Wild Things—er, monsters. I picked Salamaladder—the gecko thing—because it's really good against snakes. If the snake were to defeat my gecko, my gecko would get knocked out for 24 hours. But since my gecko defeated the snake, I get to keep the snake and use it in battles now."

"And since I'm in the game . . ."

"Anybody with a phone can battle and imprison you forever."

"Well, I would like very much for that not to happen to me."

"Right, so you need to avoid people who are playing the game."

"How do I know if someone's playing the game?"

"Well, for example, if they're walking while staring at their phone."

I squinted at him. "That's, like, everyone."

"Look, I know. It's not great, but we should mostly be able to avoid people where we're going."

"Where's that?"

Mr. Gregory smiled and leaned in. "To rescue Mark, of course."

In all the excitement about turning into a ghost, I'd totally forgotten about Mark. "Oh, that's so awesome! But how? Isn't he in another game?"

"I'll explain everything," Mr. Gregory said. "But first we've got to let your parents know you're OK."

"Oh, yeah, that's a good idea. Do you want to knock on the door and tell them? They're both in the kitchen."

"So you think it will make them feel better if a strange man knocks on their door and tells them that their missing son is OK because he's in a video game?"

"Oh, probably not. Is that why you're hiding in the bushes?"

"Part of the reason, yes. Eric plays *Go Wild*, right?"

"I'm sure he does."

"Go across the street, get his attention when he checks the game, have him call your parents, and meet me back here in 10 minutes."

"Got it."

"And Jesse?"

"Yeah?"

"Please don't let anyone else see you."

DOWNLOADING
NEXT CHAPTER...
Data Rates May Apply

CHAPTER 3
Garbage Truck

Four minutes until the bus was supposed to come, and Eric was still snoring.

"Hey." I poked Eric. Of course, my finger poked right through him. "Hey! HEY! Wake up!"

Eric made a garbage truck sound with his throat.

I threw up my hands. I'd run across the street right after my conversation with Mr. Gregory to get Eric's help. But instead of talking to him, I'd spent the last 20 minutes trying to wake him up. I tried yelling at him, blowing into his ear, even throwing that shoelace-loving ball of fur on top of him. The garbage truck kept rumbling away.

Finally, exactly 60 seconds before the bus was supposed to arrive, the truck fell off its bed.

THUD!

On the ground, Eric grunted and started putting on his socks without opening his eyes.

"Eric! Finally! I need your help!" I shouted.

He picked his nose and scratched his belly.

"Come on, come on, come on!"

He grabbed a shirt from the floor, smelled it, made a face, and threw it back. He tried another one. This one seemed acceptable. I turned my back as he changed.

"Turn on your phone! Eric, you had better not get on that bus!"

He did not turn on his phone. He did get on the bus.

After getting ready for school in less than 30 seconds, Eric stumbled downstairs, mumbled goodbye to his mom, and strapped on his book bag. He got to the corner of the street just as the bus pulled up. I looked nervously at the bus. Four out of every five kids had some sort of phone or iPod in front of their faces. How many of them were playing *Go Wild*? I looked across the street. Mr. Gregory was going nuts in the bushes.

I could ditch Eric and hope for the best. But if I did that, my parents would get real worried and call the police, and Mr. Gregory could get in trouble, and we might never get to Mark. I looked into the bus again. Even if some kids did see me in the game, they probably wouldn't notice because I'm on the bus every day anyways, right? They'd probably think I was just a regular kid going to class instead of an invisible ghost that they could capture in their phone forever.

The bus slowed to a stop. I took one last look across the street at Mr. Gregory waving his arms like crazy, then followed Eric into the bus. Eric took his usual seat toward the front, and I took my usual seat next to him. We pulled off. So far so good. Nobody was pointing yet. I sat still waiting for Eric to start fiddling with his phone. Although he had sworn off video games after the *Full Blast* incident, I knew he still played things like *Go Wild* on his phone.

"Phone games don't count," he'd told me last week.

"What do you mean they don't count? Of course they count! They're still video games!"

"No, it's only a video game if you can play it on a TV. It's even in the name—*VI-DE-O.*"

I pointed to the YouTube video he was watching on his phone at the time. He grumbled and turned away.

As Eric played with his phone on the bus, I silently thanked him for not listening to me last week. He swiped past the first page of apps, then the second, then the third and fourth and . . . how many apps could he possibly have on here? Finally, he landed on his choice for the morning.

Meow meow meow meow.

Not *Go Wild.*

Meow meow meow meow.

It looked like some weird Japanese cat game. "Eric!" I yelled, even though I knew it wouldn't do any good.

Meow meow meow.

"Eric!"

Meow.

"Eric!"

Meow.

"ERIC!"

Meow meow meow meow.

"GAAAAASP!" I heard next to me. "LOOK AT THIS!"

I slowly turned. A wide-eyed third grader across the aisle was pointing a phone directly at me and making a face like he'd just seen a ghost. I smiled and waved.

"THERE'S A KID IN THE GAME! THERE'S A KID IN THE GAME!"

I nodded and made a "this is our little secret" shushing motion.

"HEY! HEY!" The kid was desperately trying to share our secret with his seatmate. Fortunately, his buddy seemed to be more interested in catching his pre-school nap than seeing what was going on. After a few seconds of pestering, the third-grader gave up and moved on to Eric.

"HEY! HEY!"

Meow meow meow meow SPLAT!

Eric looked up.

"THERE'S SOMEONE SITTING NEXT TO YOU!"

Eric looked at the kid confused. He waved his hand through me a couple of times. "Uh, no, there's not."

"HE'S IN THE GAME! *GO WILD*!"

Eric shook his head and went back to his phone.

GASP! "I'M GOING TO CAPTURE HIM!"

Wow, that went bad in a hurry. As the kid swiped through his phone to find some horrible creature that he could use to fight me, I got right in his face. He settled on something probably with sharp teeth and brought his phone back up to . . .

"AH!" When he saw my face taking up his whole screen, the kid jumped back into his sleeping friend. His friend grunted and scrunched closer to the window.

"I need you to give the phone to him." I pointed at Eric. "NOW."

The third-grader whimpered and passed his phone to Eric. I'm guessing he'd never had a video game character demand that he give up his phone before. Eric took the phone and looked at it funny. "What is this?" he asked. "I don't . . ."

Suddenly, my face filled the screen. "Hey, I need to talk to you now."

Eric looked at the phone, then past the phone, then back at the phone. Then his mouth fell open.

"AHHHHHH!"

The whole bus turned to look at us.

CHAPTER 4

Elsa

"Stop it!" I hissed.

"AHHHHHHH!" Eric continued.

I put my hand over his mouth. That didn't do much good because my hand was, ya know, invisible. I looked up. Kids everywhere had begun recording the commotion. The third-grader across the aisle kept screaming to everyone who would listen to turn on *Go Wild*. In mere seconds, I'd be discovered by half my school. With no place to hide, I did the only thing I could think of. I climbed under the bus.

I still wasn't quite sure how the whole invisible thing worked, but I did understand that if I pushed hard enough on something, I could pass right through. So I pushed my head through the floor—which caused Eric to scream louder—

"AHHHHHHH!"

And found a good place to sit under the bus. I mean, it wasn't a "good" place. It was rumbly and rusty and kind of hot. But there was enough room for me to curl up once I pushed the rest of my body through. The last thing I did before disappearing down there for good was poke my head back up through the floor and try to explain the situation to Eric one more time.

"Hey, I'm OK, but I need you to call my parents to tell them . . ."

"AHHHHHHH!" Eric's eyes got bigger and his face got redder as he stared through the phone at the talking head on the ground.

"You know what? Never mind." I disappeared back under the bus, where I stayed for the rest of the ride to school. While I probably wouldn't recommend riding under the bus every day, as a one-time ghost thing, it actually turned out to be not too bad.

When we finally arrived at school, I rolled off my perch under the bus and scanned the crowd walking into school. No Eric. Had he already gone inside? Oh no, there he was, spinning around in circles with a phone in front of his face. I stepped out and waved to him. He stopped spinning, waved back, and jogged over.

"Jesse! Is it really you?!"

"Yeah, I need . . ."

"Oh, cooooool!" Eric looked me up and down with his phone. "After you crawled under the bus, I figured out that you'd probably gotten sucked into another game. How is it? Is it the best?"

"It's OK; I just need . . ."

"Can I come, too? How do I get in?"

"I don't think you can. What you can do is . . ."

"Have you upgraded yet?"

"I don't know what that means. But I need you to . . ."

"HEY! You haven't seen a Golden Hawkadoodle have you? They're super rare, but I hear there's one around here! If you . . ."

"ERIC!"

"What?"

"I need you to call my parents to let them know I'm OK."

"Yeah, sure. Why didn't you just say so?"

I walked around the corner of the school with Eric as he called my mom. "Hi, Mrs. Rigsby . . . Oh yeah, as a matter of fact, he's right here! Yeah, he, uh, he came over to my house early this morning . . . Why didn't he tell you he was coming over? I don't know; that seems irresponsible."

I gave him a look and threw up my hands. Of course, he couldn't see.

"Sure, you can talk to him!" Eric held out the phone. I stared at him in disbelief. After a second of holding his phone in midair, Eric realized his mistake and took it back. "Actually, sorry, he can't talk right now. Uh-huh. OK. I'll let him know."

He hung up, went back to *Go Wild*, and turned the phone toward me. "Your mom said you're in big trouble."

"Thanks."

"Well, you should have told her where you were going."

"I'll remember that next time I get sucked into a video game."

"A mobile game."

"A what?"

"You got sucked into a mobile game. A video game is one you play on a . . ."

"OK, we don't need to go through this again. I just need to get out of here before anyone else sees me."

"Where are you going?"

"To rescue Mark."

Eric gasped. "Really?! How?"

"I don't have time to explain," I said. Mostly because I didn't know.

"Well, as long as you're in the game, you should figure out your special ability."

"I don't think I have a special ability."

"Sure you do! Every Wild Thing has a special ability. Like there's one that can call down lightning, there's one that has poison burps, one that does tornadoes."

"I don't think I can do any of those things."

"Well, you can probably do something. You should try figuring it out. While you're at it, maybe you could sneak into the cafeteria and let me know what's for dessert today."

"I'm not doing that."

"Fine, but if you happen to see a Golden Hawkadoodle . . ."

"Just go to class."

Eric gave me a thumbs-up and put his phone in his pocket. Then he looked back in my direction and waved his hand where he remembered my face being. "Man, this is cool!" Eric exclaimed as he turned to walk to class.

Alone at last, I took a breath and looked around. Mr. Gregory had seen me get on the bus, so he'd probably be at the school soon. All I had to do was stay away from anyone playing *Go Wild* until then. In the meantime . . . I looked at my hands. Did I really have special powers? I squinted really hard and tried to shoot fire from my eyes like the snake. Nothing happened. I burped. Smelly but not poisonous. I pressed my finger against my palm like Spider-Man, got mad like the Hulk, and clenched my fists like Wolverine. Zip, zero, nada.

This was stupid. After being up for half the night, I needed a nap, not a superpower. I yawned and stretched my arms.

SWOOOOOOOOOSH!

The tree next to me turned into a giant block of ice.

Whoooaaaaa. What was that? I tried yawning again. Nothing happened. I stretched my arm again. Nothing. But when I stretched my arms and spread out my fingers—

SWOOOOOOOOOSH!

A blast of ice shot out of my hand. Nice! I tried it again.

SWOOOOOOOOOSH!

OK, so I was basically Elsa from *Frozen*! Maybe I could build an ice castle next to the school. I pointed my hand to the sky and iced again.

SWOOOOOOOOOOSH!

SQUAWK!

CRASH!

What was that? I ran over to find that I'd accidentally blasted a big golden bird out of the sky. It fell to the ground in a chunk of ice.

"HEY! What did you do to the Hawkadoodle?!"

"Nothing! I thought your Blastasaurus got him!"

Two girls appeared from around the corner of the school. They were accompanied by their Wild Things— one had a spiky T. rex–looking monster, and the other had a brown version of the Bigfoot I'd seen earlier in my tub. As soon as they rounded the corner, they stopped dead in their tracks. They looked through their phones first at the Golden Hawkadoodle at my feet and then at me.

"Jesse?" one of them said.

That's when the T. rex charged.

CHAPTER 5
Slip 'N Slide

"ROOOOOOOOOAR!"

That was the T. rex.

"GRRRROWLLLLL!"

That was the Bigfoot.

"HELLLLLLLLLP!"

That was me.

We all ran toward the basketball courts, me leading the way and my two monster friends following close behind. As they gained ground, I remembered my power. I reached back, spread my fingers, and . . .

SWOOOOOOOOOSH!

. . . A big ol' miss. I tried again.

SWOOOOOOOOOSH!

I froze the flagpole behind Bigfoot. One more time.

SWOOOOOOOOOSH!

I missed again, but this time I missed in front of the monsters instead of behind them, creating a frozen Slip 'N Slide on the ground.

THUD-THUD-THUD-ROOOOOOOAAAA-THUNK.

The T. rex slipped, then slid across the ice, wildly waving its tiny T. rex arms to regain its balance. It spun around a few times before smacking its head into a tree. I looked back to see it lying on the ground with stars floating above its head.

One down! By now, the Bigfoot was almost on top of me. I reached back and tried icing again.

SWOOOWWwwwrrrr.

Instead of the usual ice blast, my hand spit out a pathetic snowball. It hit the monster in the face, freezing half its mouth in a permanent sneer, while the other half continued to growl. I reached back to ice again.

Click. Click. Click.

My hand actually clicked. I guess that meant I was out of ice. I circled around and ran back toward my Slip 'N Slide. By the time I reached the dinosaur,

Bigfoot was swiping at my head. I jumped onto the ice, slid for 10 feet, and turned to see how Bigfoot had done. Unfortunately, he turned out to be a little more coordinated than the T. rex. After shuffling his feet and spinning a few times, he eventually recovered to resume the chase. I ran past the girls, who had been staring at the scene through their phones with their mouths open the whole time.

"PLEASE, CAN YOU TELL YOUR MONSTER TO STOP CHASING ME? THANK YOU!" I screamed as I passed by. They continued their unhelpful open-mouthed stare.

I sprinted past them toward the school and then *POP!* through the wall into the school library. Just before the Bigfoot followed me in, I dove behind a row of encyclopedias in the reference section. The Bigfoot snorted a few times. I don't think he saw me. I took a second to catch my breath.

Well, if there's one good place to hide in the library, it's the encyclopedia section. Judging by the dust on these things, not a single person has touched an encyclopedia since the Internet was invented. The uninterrupted wall of books provided some nice cover for me to take a little rest.

"And over here are our reference books."

I scrunched behind the E-G section as a librarian led a teenage girl into my aisle.

"You won't have to do much here. Just make sure everything stays neat. This is the one area where you'll have to dust every few months. See?" The librarian bent down, removed two of the encyclopedias I was hiding behind, and wiped her finger along the shelf. "It gets a little dusty."

Are you kidding me?! Out of all the books to pick up! I tried rolling to better cover, but I was too late. Bigfoot saw me.

"GROWWWWWWWWWL!"

I got up and ran, plowing through bookshelf after bookshelf until I popped out of the back of the library into the cafeteria. The Bigfoot followed close behind. As I ran past the lunch ladies setting out trays of food, I peeked over. Peach cobbler for dessert. Eric wouldn't be happy.

I ran through the cafeteria into a classroom, where nobody noticed me except for one very surprised kid who had been hiding his phone at his desk playing *Go Wild*. He jumped when he saw a sixth-grader followed by a giant Bigfoot burst through the chalkboard. I swerved into the hallway and continued trying to shake the monster.

I needed a plan fast. The end of the hallway was coming up, and it dead-ended into a pair of doors. Maybe if I dove through the door on the right and quickly rolled through the wall into the room on the left, I could get away. I put my head down and sprinted faster. I could practically feel Bigfoot's breath on my neck—20 yards, 10 yards, almost there. I looked up to judge the dive, and only then did I realize which door I was about to jump through.

THE GIRLS' BATHROOM?!

Invisible or not, no way I was diving headfirst into the girls' bathroom. I jabbed my right foot into the ground to switch directions on the fly. Unfortunately, doing anything "on the fly" requires a bit of coordination, and coordination is not something I was born with. My legs twisted into a pretzel, causing me to trip and roll to a stop right outside the bathroom door.

"GROWWWWWWWWWL!"

I put my hands in front of my face and prepared to get eaten.

"GROWWWWWWWWWL!"

I scrunched into a ball.

"GROWWWWWWWWWL!"

Was this monster ever going to eat me? I peeked between my fingers to see the Bigfoot leaned all the way over with its arms stretched toward me. The monster scraped its feet on the ground and clawed wildly, kind of like a dog at the end of its leash trying to catch a taunting squirrel. I quickly rolled into the boys' bathroom and sprawled out on the tile floor to catch my breath. What was that all about?

"BRAWWWWWWW!"

Unfortunately, I didn't have time to figure it out, because at that moment something that looked exactly like a *Jurassic Park* velociraptor stepped onto my chest.

CHAPTER 6
Got Him

The lights in the room dimmed, and intense battle music started playing.

"BRAWWWWWWW!"

"Hey! Wait!" I scrambled to my feet.

The velociraptor stepped back and got into a fighting stance.

"Jesse?"

I spun around. Stu Sullinger, a kinda tall, kinda dumb kid from my class, was looking at me through his phone with a bewildered expression on his face.

"Stu! Stu, you gotta help me!"

"Whoaaaaa!"

The velociraptor swiped at my face. I dodged left.

"How did Jesse make himself a character in the game?!"

"I'm not a character in the game! I *AM* in the game!"

The velociraptor swiped again. I dodged right.

"Is this yours?!" I pointed at the velociraptor.

"Wait," Stu said. "No way! Are you talking to me?"

"BECAUSE IT WOULD BE REALLY GREAT IF YOU COULD TELL IT TO STOP!" I said as the velociraptor climbed onto the counter.

"Ha ha, this is nuts! Jesse's going to have to show me how to do this!"

"BRAWWWWWWW!"

The velociraptor launched itself at me with its claws out. I rolled underneath the attack.

"STUUUUUUUU!"

"He's going to go crazy when he finds out that I captured his character!"

"What? No! Hey, are you even listening to me?!"

Stu swiped on his phone a few times, and the velociraptor's eyes turned glowing red. It crouched down and started snorting like a bull. This might be a good time to try the ice thing again. I stretched out my hand and . . .

SWOOwwrr.

... lobbed a pathetic, slushy snowball at the dinosaur's face. Apparently, my power needed longer than three minutes to recharge.

"BRAWWWWWWW!"

The velociraptor put its head down and charged. I tried to jump out of the way, but I was too late. It head-butted me through the toilet stall door.

"Oof!" I landed on the floor and bonked my head on the toilet. As the velociraptor collected itself, I tried to find something to use as protection. Maybe I could climb through the toilet?

"BRAWWWWWWW!"

I did not get to test that horrible idea, because right then, the velociraptor pounced its final pounce. I squeezed my eyes closed. Suddenly, the screeching stopped. The battle music stopped. Everything got dead quiet. I finally dared to open my eyes.

All I could see was Stu's face. He looked like a 100-foot-tall giant. From this angle, I was getting a particularly good view of his right nostril. Stu looked down at me and broke into a huge smile.

"GOT HIM!"

DOWNLOADING NEXT CHAPTER...
Data Rates May Apply

CHAPTER 7

Upside Down Flamezoid

"HEY! LET ME OUT! THIS ISN'T A GAME! STU! STU? STUUUUUUUU!"

My screaming did no good, mostly because I'm not even sure that I was screaming. I seemed to be frozen in place inside of Stu's phone with my mouth gaping open and fist in the air.

"You look just like Jesse!" Stu said.

"I AM JESSE!" I tried to scream.

Stu reached down and clicked off his phone. As soon as he did, the lights went out all around me, and I dropped to the ground. I stayed that way in the dark for a second, and then a dim night-light clicked on. After my eyes adjusted, I found that I was trapped inside a big clear cube, surrounded by a sea of similar cubes, all floating in space. Is this what the inside of a phone looks like? I felt a tap on my shoulder.

"What is . . . AHHHHHHHH!"

I turned to see the velociraptor staring at me. "Braw?" it said with its head tilted.

"DON'T EAT ME!" I yelled as I backed toward the corner.

"Braw?" the velociraptor said again. It started walking around me and sniffing. I stood perfectly still. It seemed particularly interested in the part of my head that I'd hit on the toilet. It stopped there and tapped. "Braw?" it said again.

Whatever it was doing, it didn't seem too interested in eating me. In fact, if I had to guess, I'd say that it was asking if I was OK.

"Uh, yeah, it's OK," I said to the dinosaur creature that definitely couldn't understand English.

"Braw!" it replied and rubbed me with its nose. It then tilted its head down in front of me and closed its eyes. Uhhhh, OK? We stood that way in silence for a little bit. After a few seconds, it nudged my hand with its snout and put its head down again.

I scratched the velociraptor's head between its eyes. "Is this what you want?"

The dinosaur leaned into the scratch and its tail like a dog. Finally, it licked me with dinosaur tongue and bounded off into the darkn

I sat down in my corner of the glass cube. N what? How would anyone find me in here? How lon would I have to be missing for Stu to figure out that he'd captured the real Jesse into his phone? What would happen to Mark in the meantime? While all these thoughts swirled in my head, I fell asleep.

"Yeah, he was in the bathroom!" Stu said. I popped awake. "I'm telling you, it looked exactly like him. Look, I'll show you."

Suddenly, the lights came back on, and I felt myself get sucked back into the air. Stu and his buddies appeared in front of me. It looked like we were in the cafeteria.

"Doesn't it look like him?"

"Ha ha, yeah, he's got that same goofy hair and big nose!"

OK, guys, really?

"That's pretty cool! How do you make your own character in the game?"

"I don't know," Stu said. "I've been trying to find Jesse all morning to ask him myself. Oh, wait, there's his friend. Hey, Eric!"

I saw Eric appear behind Stu's shoulder. "What?"

"Do you know where Jesse is?"

"Mmmhmmm," Eric said while nodding his head. Then he caught himself and started shaking his head. "I mean no. Nooooooo. Uh, I mean kind of. Well, you see . . . " Eric is so bad at lying.

"If you do see him, let him know that I want to find out how he did this," Stu showed Eric the screen with my body frozen in place.

Eric glanced at the screen and nodded. Then he did a double take. "WHOA! Is that . . . Where did you find him?!"

"He just showed up in the bathroom. My Sliceasaurus took him out in, like, five seconds."

Eric started pacing. "This is not good! THIS IS NOT GOOD!"

"Stop being weird, man. It's just a game."

"No, it's not! I mean, yes, it is, of course it is, but oh boy. Boy oh boy. Hey, why don't you let him go? Have you ever thought of letting him go?"

"Dude, you know how this works. Once you capture a Wild Thing, you can't just put it back."

"But I can fight you for him! Let's duel Wild Things!"

"No way! I'm keeping him forever!"

"Come on, I'm sure I have something you'd want. Look." Eric took out his phone and started scrolling through Wild Things. "Freezard, Newtonium, Slaptopus . . ." He skipped past one without mentioning it. "Starmander, Dragonfish . . ."

"Hey, wait, what was that one?" Stu asked.

"Oh, that's a Level 3 Starmander! Pretty sweet, huh?"

"No, the one before."

"What, oh, uh, that's nothing. That's just . . ."

Stu grabbed the phone and scrolled back. "An Upside Down Flamezoid? You have an Upside Down Flamezoid?! I don't know anyone who has an Upside Down Flamezoid!"

Eric snatched his phone back. "Oh yeah, no big deal. But anyways, if you want any of these other ones."

"No way, I want to fight the Upside Down Flamezoid."

"Can I interest you in a Fluffy Chupachu?"

I wanted to jump out of the phone and strangle Eric. Just get me out of here!

"Upside Down Flamezoid or nothing."

"I'm sorry, I can't . . ."

"Bye." Stu started walking away.

ERIC!

"Wait! OK. I'll do it. But no attack boosters."

"Deal!" Stu grinned and swiped in front of my face a few times. Suddenly, I teleported out of the phone and back into the school. I found myself face-to-face with a big, black bat that had no eyes. The lights dimmed. The music started.

The bat opened its gigantic mouth and let out a deafening *SCREEEEEEECH!* When the screech reached its loudest pitch, a flame shot out of its mouth.

"AH!" I rolled left. The floor where I'd been standing was now a charred hole in the ground.

"Wow! Jesse must really want to live in your phone forever!" Eric said, clearly for my benefit.

So to be rescued, I'd have to get flamed to death by a giant, angry bat? This seemed like a horrible deal!

"Let's see if you can dodge this!" Stu shouted. He swiped his phone, and I got struck with a lightning bolt.

"Ouch!" Everything flashed white. When the world came back into focus, I was looking down on Eric and his bat from my new height of 12 feet tall.

"I said no attack boosters!" Eric yelped.

"Oops," Stu said.

Stu swiped a few more times, and I felt my hand start tingling. Oh no. Oh nonono. My left hand began rising on its own. NONONO! I tried pushing it down with my other hand, but I was too late.

SWOOOOOOOOOOSH!

I shot a massive blast of ice at the bat. The bat jumped into the air and did a barrel roll to dodge, but the ice blast was too big—I scored a direct hit on its right wing. The bat screeched and fell to the ground with one wing encased in ice.

"Ha ha!" Stu tapped a few times, and I started walking toward the struggling creature. I tried with all my might to stop my feet from walking, but the best I could do was slow myself to an awkward shuffle. The bat tried limping away, but mostly it just flopped in place. I felt a tingle in my left hand again. Oh man, if I iced this bat, Stu would win and I'd be trapped inside his phone forever.

"Watch out!" I yelled. Just two feet away now. The bat looked more pathetic than ever. My hand started rising. "Eric!" I yelled. "Tell Mr. Gregory I'm sorry!" The tingle in my hand turned into a buzzing. This was it.

At that moment, the bat turned to me, smiled a toothy smile, opened its giant mouth, and swallowed me whole.

CHAPTER 8

The Leash

"GOT HIM!"

"Oh, come on! That's not fair!"

Eric didn't hear Stu's whining because he was too busy dancing in place. After a full minute of whooping and belly wiggling, Eric finally remembered that his best friend was inside his phone. A few taps and swipes later, I fell onto the cafeteria floor.

"You are the worst!" I yelled as soon as I hit the ground.

Eric looked puzzled. "What, I rescued you, right?"

"After getting real close to letting me die inside a phone for some stupid bat!"

"Well, technically, it's not a bat . . ."

I turned and walked away.

"Hey, Jesse, wait! Come back!"

No way. I was getting out of this school before some other dumb monster started chasing me. As soon as I found Mr. Gregory, I'd stick by his side like glue and . . .

"Oof!"

Just as I took my first step out of the cafeteria, I felt a tug on my chest. I tried to take another step. Stuck. I turned to Eric, who was still looking at me through his phone in the middle of the cafeteria. "Wanna tell me what this is about?!" I yelled.

Eric glanced around and walked over to me. "Yeah," he whispered as he turned the corner with me. "You're on a leash."

"A what?"

"Once you capture a Wild Thing, you can let it out on a leash to chase and battle other Wild Things, but you can never set it free again."

"But what about those girls' Bigfoot and T. rex that were chasing me earlier? They certainly didn't seem to be on a leash."

Eric sighed and acted like he was explaining things to a two-year-old. "You can make your leash a lot longer if you want to pay money. But even the longest leash will always run out of line."

I remembered the Bigfoot straining and clawing at me by the bathrooms. "So we're stuck together?"

Eric shrugged.

"Terrific. Well, can you at least pay to get a longer leash so I don't have to stay so close to you?"

"No can do. My mom took her credit card number off my phone a loooooong time ago."

We stood in silence for a few seconds. "Well, there is one adult who might be able to help us," I said.

We sneaked outside the school to look for Mr. Gregory. I figured he must be here by now, probably hiding in a . . .

"Psst!" the bush next to the dumpsters whispered. We walked over. Mr. Gregory poked his head out with a phone in front of his face. "Thank goodness you're OK!" he said to me. He turned to Eric. "Thank you so much for keeping him safe—you have no idea how important he is for rescuing Mark. Don't worry; Jesse and I will be back with Mark in just a few hours."

"Cool," Eric said. "But, um, one thing. Can we borrow your credit card first?"

"Why would you need a credit card?"

"Leash reasons."

"Leash reasons?" Mr. Gregory started to get panicky. "What do you mean leash reasons?!"

"Well, technically—don't get mad—but technically, Jesse kind of got himself captured, but it's OK cuz I rescued him, but it's also kind of not OK cuz now he can only walk around on a short leash."

Mr. Gregory turned his phone to me with big eyes. "YOU GOT CAPTURED?!"

"I said not to get mad," Eric said.

"This is not good! This is not good at all!"

"It'll be fine if you just let me borrow your credit card," Eric said.

"I DON'T HAVE A CREDIT CARD!" Mr. Gregory yelled.

"Oh, I just thought since you're an adult . . ."

"I mean, I have a credit card, but I can't use it because they'll find me!"

"Who's 'they'?" I asked, suddenly aware of the possibility that a full-grown man who constantly hides in bushes might be crazy.

"Bionosoft!" Mr. Gregory hissed.

"Uh, the video game company?" Eric asked.

"Wait, is that why you're hiding in bushes?" I asked.

"Listen," Mr. Gregory whispered. "They are doing some very bad things over there. VERY bad things! If they ever found out what I was up to . . ."

Eric glanced in my direction with an "Are we sure this guy is OK?" look on his face.

Mr. Gregory noticed the look. "This sounds crazy, right? It probably sounds crazy."

Eric laughed nervously while backing up ever so slightly. "Heh heh heh. Crazy? That's funny. We don't think you're crazy. Right, Jesse?"

"Everything is just, well, it's honestly a little hard to believe," I said.

"Just like it might be hard for someone to believe that you're in a video game right now?" Mr. Gregory asked.

I shrugged.

"Mark is trapped inside of Bionosoft. I've seen him with my own eyes," Mr. Gregory explained. "Now you can believe that or not—that's up to you. But there's, um, there's one other thing I need to tell you."

I had a sick feeling in my stomach. "What?"

"The only way I can get you out of *Go Wild* is by sneaking you into Bionosoft."

**DOWNLOADING
NEXT CHAPTER...**
Data Rates May Apply

CHAPTER 9

Ice Bazooka

Crazy or not, Mr. Gregory was my only hope for getting out of this video game alive, which is why Eric and I soon found ourselves trudging through the woods behind our school.

"How much farther?" Eric whined after 15 minutes.

"Not too far," Mr. Gregory lied. We hiked for another hour before Mr. Gregory motioned for Eric to be quiet. He then pointed to an office built into the hill in front of us.

"Whoooaaaaaa," Eric whispered.

I always kind of assumed that video game companies worked in sweet offices with Ping-Pong tables and old arcade games and cardboard cutouts of Sonic the Hedgehog everywhere. While some video game companies might operate that way, Bionosoft did not seem to be one of them. The building in front of us looked more like a top-secret government facility that experiments on sheep. The building was big, black, and windowless. Scary warning signs and an electric fence surrounded the whole thing.

"How are we supposed to get in there?!" I asked as we approached the fence.

"*We* weren't supposed to. The plan was for you to sneak in as the invisible kid while I helped you with a laptop I'd hidden in the woods," Mr. Gregory said. "But now that we have to get both of you in, I'm out of ideas."

I looked down the fence at a guardhouse 30 yards away. "Maybe we don't have to both sneak in," I said. "How long is the longest leash?"

"Four hundred yards," Mr. Gregory said.

I nodded. "Follow me." I led everyone toward the guardhouse. As soon as a car pulled up and the security guy walked to the window, I motioned for Eric to follow me and crouch-sprinted to the little building. We sat on the ground next to the guardhouse, me planning my next move and Eric trying to wheeze quieter.

"OK, pull up the credit card screen in *Go Wild* and be ready," I said. "I'm gonna try to do something, but I don't know if it'll work."

Eric nodded, still panting.

I gave him a thumbs-up and rolled through the guardhouse wall. There was the security guy, sitting at a desk in front of a panel of camera monitors. I took a deep breath and walked up to him. This was going to be super weird. I crawled underneath his chair and slowly pushed my head up. *Pop!* I made it through the chair and now sat face-to-face with the guy's large, khaki-clad bottom. OK, this next part would be the trickiest. I located the back pocket and pushed my head ever so slightly until . . . *Pop!* My face made it through the pocket. My eyeball was now smooshed up against what I'd come for—the guy's wallet. I pushed forward one more time. *Pop!* I could see inside his wallet! And once

I took a few seconds to focus my eyes, I could even read the numbers on the credit card! I took a full minute to memorize the whole thing—I never, ever wanted to do this again. Once I'd repeated the number back to myself a few times, I ran back to Eric.

"5199-7455 . . ." I recited a long string of numbers as Eric typed.

"OK," he said once we'd finished. "What's the CVV code?"

"The CVV code? What's a CVV code?!"

"How am I supposed to know? I'm not the one with the credit card! Oh, wait, it says here that it's a three-digit number on the back."

I sighed and walked back into the guardhouse to look through the security guy's wallet again. A minute later, I returned. "It's 455. Also, I accidentally learned the color of his underwear if you want to know that, too."

Eric put the number in the phone. "That worked!"

"So how much does it cost to make the leash as long as possible?" I asked as we scrambled away. "Like two or three bucks?"

"Uhhh," Eric scrolled through his options. "The Ultimate Leash is $49.99."

"Dollars?!"

"Well, yeah, it's 400 yards long."

"You're telling me that a fake, invisible leash inside a video game costs 50 real dollars?"

"I mean, it's the only way you're gonna catch any of the faster Wild Things."

I shook my head. Eric swiped a few times, and I heard a very appropriate *cha-ching* cash register sound.

"OK, your leash is upgraded now," he said. "But if you're going in there by yourself, we should probably get you powered up."

"Really? It's not like I'm going to be fighting my way in or anything. It seems like monsters in the wild are peaceful until something attacks them, right?"

Eric didn't answer because he was too busy spending someone else's money. "Level 3? Check." *Cha-ching!* "Ice bazooka? Why not?" *Cha-ching!* "Twice-as-nice ice, battle blizzard, frosty fingers . . ." *Cha-ching, cha-ching, cha-ching!*

My whole body started tingling. "Eric!"

He finally looked up.

"How much did all of that cost?!"

He looked back at the phone. "Like $70."

"ERIC!"

"You want to do cool ice stuff, right?"

"I wanted to pay him back!"

"Oh."

We finally made it back to Mr. Gregory. "Can we borrow $120?" Eric asked.

"Yeah, sure," Mr. Gregory said, clearly not listening. He was typing on the laptop he'd hidden in the woods outside of Bionosoft. "Come on, come on, come on . . . yes!" Right then, a glowing pair of glasses popped out of Mr. Gregory's computer in the same way that the pear had popped out of his phone earlier that morning.

"Put those on," he said to me.

I bent down and grabbed them. They were definitely in the game and not real life because they didn't slip through my hands when I picked them up off the ground.

I put them on and noticed they seemed a little heavy. "What do these do?"

"Come look!" Mr. Gregory said. Eric and I gathered around the computer. On the screen, Mr. Gregory had pulled up live video from the view of my glasses. "When you're wearing those, we can see and hear everything you're experiencing in the game, and we can also communicate with you through an earpiece built into the frame."

"But how?!" I asked. "The glasses aren't even real!"

"I worked on this game! I know a few hacks." Mr. Gregory smiled, clearly quite proud of himself.

"Sweet!" Eric said. "Can we have that $120 now?"

"One hundred twenty dollars?!" Mr. Gregory said with his eyes bugging out of his head.

After Eric finished explaining that we needed the money for "leash reasons" and also how cool and necessary the ice bazooka was, Mr. Gregory finally got some cash out of his wallet, but not before making us promise that we wouldn't spend any more money. We decided to test our new system on the guard. I walked into the guardhouse. "Can you see him?" I whispered.

"Yes," Mr. Gregory said. "And talk louder. It's OK; he can't hear you."

I watched the guard do boring guard things—look at the monitors, check his watch, yawn. Then he picked up his phone and started texting.

"Now!" I yelled.

Just then, Eric ran out of the woods with two balled-up bills, threw them into the guardhouse—

PLOP PLOP.

—and ran back behind cover. When the guard heard the bills hit the ground behind him, he walked over to investigate. His eyes got huge when he picked up a $100 and a $20.

"Success!" I yelled and got out of there.

Back in the woods, Mr. Gregory gave me a thumbs-up. "Excellent work, Jesse. Now it's time to find Mark." He pulled up an overhead view of the Bionosoft building on his computer. "OK, here's where we are. You'll go through this fence and follow the road to Bionosoft's truck-loading dock. Once you get inside, I'll direct you over the earpiece."

"Got it," I said. "But what if I run into any monsters?"

"It's fine," Mr. Gregory said. "Any Wild Thing you come across should truly be wild, so they won't attack."

"And if they do attack, unleash the ice bazooka!" Eric said.

"No ice bazooka!" Mr. Gregory warned. "The last thing we need is for you to get into a fight!"

"Agree to disagree," Eric mumbled.

I took a deep breath. "Got it. Thanks for all your help, Mr. Gregory."

"Jesse." Mr. Gregory got all serious. "Be careful in there. We can't lose both of you."

I nodded and walked through the forest toward the fence. Not "through the forest" like a normal person but "through the forest" as in through every tree I could find. It was very cool. I passed through the fence, pushed through some bushes, and . . .

Uh-oh.

"Are you guys seeing this?" I asked over the earpiece. Between me and Bionosoft was a field filled with Wild Things. But these Wild Things weren't wandering around peacefully like the ones I'd seen outside my house that morning. They were flexing and pacing and hissing, and every single one of them had glowing red attack eyes.

"ICE BAZOOKA!" Eric said over the earpiece.

Mr. Gregory came on. "Don't move!"

"Why are they all in attack mode?!"

He sighed. "Bionosoft must have known we were coming. Abort mission."

"But . . ."

Right then, I felt a claw slowly run down my back. I turned to see a velociraptor with glowing red eyes and sharp teeth smiling an evil smile.

CHAPTER 10

Vinnie

"ICE BAZOOKA!"

"RUN AWAY!"

Eric and Mr. Gregory were both giving terrible advice. The ice bazooka would serve as a personal invitation to every Wild Thing on the lawn to attack at once. Running would get me about two steps before being devoured by a hungry dinosaur. The rest of the world went dim, and battle music started playing. I sized up the velociraptor in front of me.

"BRAWWWWWWW!"

This one was even bigger and scarier than Stu's. "Hey, buddy," I tried.

"BRAWWWWWWWW!"

That seemed to make him angrier. "I'd like to be friends," I continued.

"HE DOES NOT WANT TO BE YOUR FRIEND!" Eric yelled over the earpiece.

"My name is Jesse. Can I call you Vinnie? Vinnie the velociraptor?" I reached out my hand. The dinosaur snapped a few times, but I didn't pull away. Instead, I gave it a head scratch.

"Braw?" The dinosaur tilted its head and wagged its tail a little bit. Its eyes flickered from glowing red to light brown. It then shook its head and let out another long "BRAWWWWWW!"

"JESSE, WHAT ARE YOU DOING?!" I heard over the earpiece.

I continued scratching the velociraptor between the eyes, and the tail wagging returned. The dinosaur nuzzled its nose into my chest and actually began thumping its back leg. It eventually rolled onto its back, causing the battle music to stop and the darkness to lift. "That's a good boy," I said.

"Braw!" Vinnie cooed back.

"I've never seen anything like that," Mr. Gregory marveled over the earpiece.

"I have," I said. After a few minutes of head scratching and belly rubbing, I looked the dinosaur in the eye. "Can you help me get in there?" I asked.

"Braw!"

"You know it can't understand you," Eric said over the radio.

"Velociraptors are smart!" I said. "I've seen *Jurassic Park.*"

"That's not a velociraptor; it's a Sliceasaurus," Eric said.

"Same difference." I turned back to Vinnie. "So whaddya say, buddy?"

The velociraptor (I'm not calling it a Sliceasaurus; that's ridiculous) jumped to its feet and bounded around me.

"Ha ha! Let's go!" I climbed onto its back and pointed to the loading dock. Vinnie nodded and took off. The army of Wild Things on the Bionosoft lawn all looked up at once. Maybe this wasn't the best idea? The first to greet us was a line of half-metal robot lizards.

"Point your fist at them and squeeze!" Mr. Gregory said over the radio.

WASWOOSH!

A laser beam of ice exploded out of my hand and blasted through every lizard, freezing them in place.

"WOO-HOO! ICE BAZOOKA!" Eric yelled.

I didn't have time to celebrate, because a green rhinoceros with an extra-long, extra-sharp horn galloped up on my right.

"Squeeze your right hand like you're holding a sword!" Mr. Gregory offered.

SHHHHING!

An ice sword appeared in my hand. The rhinoceros tried to spear me with its horn, but I blocked it with the sword. We went back and forth sword fighting, him with his razor horn and me with my icicle, for a few seconds before—*SHING!*—I cut off the horn and—*SWOOSH!*—froze the rhino.

"AHH!" I slapped at my head. Something big and feathery had swooped down and was trying to lift me off of Vinnie.

"Grab it and squeeze!"

I did as the voice in my ear instructed. The huge bird froze in my hand.

"FROSTY FINGERS!" Eric celebrated over the radio.

Vinnie had to bob and weave across the lawn and up the hill to avoid all the attacks, but we were now only 10 yards away from the loading dock. Unfortunately, a mob of angry creatures had formed behind us, and they were gaining fast. I turned around and iced the ground behind me.

SWOOOOOOSH!

I iced and iced until I'd formed an enormous frozen lake. The first Wild Thing—a massive white bear—stepped onto the ice and promptly wiped out on its face. That caused the man-sized walking stick behind it to trip, which made a spiky, rolling thing tip over, which caused a 20–Wild Thing pileup on the ice. Vinnie and I broke through the loading dock door, leaving the wreckage behind.

"Where to now?" I yelled over the earpiece.

"Straight through the warehouse," Mr. Gregory said. "All the way in the back is a door that leads to the main building. Get there before that pileup sorts itself out."

I pushed Vinnie toward the back of the dark warehouse, but he wouldn't budge. "Come on, we gotta move!" He backed up a little. "Let's go!" He made a tiny whimpering noise. After a few seconds of kicking and prodding, I finally gave up and jumped off. "Look, there's nothing to worry about," I said as I stepped right into the waiting claw of a giant black bat.

"AHHHHHHH!"

An Upside Down Flamezoid rocketed me up into the warehouse rafters. By the time I got my bearings, I was hanging upside down 50 feet in the air.

"SCREEEE . . ." the bat began its flaming death screech.

"Guys? GUYS, WHAT DO I DO NOW?!" I yelled over my earpiece.

"EEEEEEEEEE . . ." the bat continued.

"This is so bad!" Eric yelled.

"You can try . . ."

"EEEEEEEEEECH!" The Upside Down Flamezoid cut off Mr. Gregory mid-suggestion by finishing its screech and shooting fire out of its mouth at me. I put up my hand in defense and ice blasted the wall of flame. The fire and ice met in the middle, causing a waterfall to start pouring from the warehouse rafters. We fought each other to a draw for a few moments before running out of power at the same time. We both breathed heavily as we determined our next moves. Then the bat remembered that, oh yeah, it could just eat me alive. It opened its giant mouth, but just as it started shoving me inside—*WHOP!*—it got smacked in the face with an egg.

The Upside Down Flamezoid grunted. *WHOP!* Another egg. It let out a series of high-pitched noises to find the egg thrower with its bat sonar. I looked down and discovered the source of the irritation at the same time the bat did. Vinnie! He was holding an egg in one hand and what appeared to be a baby bat in his mouth.

"SCREEEEEEECH!" The bat dropped me and took off for Vinnie, presenting a good news/bad news situation. Good news: The giant death bat no longer wanted to swallow me whole. Yay! Bad news: Getting flattened on a cement floor is arguably less fun than being eaten alive by a bat.

As I tumbled through the air, I screamed and waved my outstretched arms.

SWOOOOOSH!

Twenty feet, 10 feet—I braced for impact. But the impact never came. Instead, I temporarily picked up speed before finally sliding to a stop at the far end of the warehouse. It turns out my desperate icing combined with the wild tumbling worked together to create the happy accident of an ice ramp on the ground that not only broke my fall but also spit me out where I wanted to go! Just one problem . . .

"SCREEEEEEEE . . ."

I turned back toward Vinnie and the Upside Down Flamezoid across the warehouse. Vinnie retreated while the bat built its flame.

"VINNIE!" I yelled.

He shooed me toward the door I needed to go through with his skinny dinosaur arms. At that moment, the army of Wild Things from outside started pouring through the wall behind him.

"I'M COMING FOR YOU!" I got only two steps toward my dinosaur friend before the screeching reached its highest point, and the bat unleashed a wall of fire, engulfing Vinnie and the rest of the Wild Things behind him.

CHAPTER 11
Ground Control

The flaming lasted 10 full seconds before the bat paused to reload.

"VINNIE!" I yelled.

The bat looked at me.

"Get out of there!" Mr. Gregory said.

I turned and ran as the bat started another death screech. "Can you bring Vinnie back?!" I asked.

"I'm sorry. That's not the way it works," Mr. Gregory said.

"Bring him back!" I yelled while fighting back tears. "You made this game. You can bring him back!"

"I'm sorry. I really am," Mr. Gregory said. "But we need you to refocus."

"But . . ."

"Mark needs you to refocus."

I slowed down and took a few deep breaths.

"That's it," Mr. Gregory said. "Now I need you to walk straight down the hallway you're in. At the end of the hall, you'll find an elevator that goes all the way to the basement."

Sniff, sniff. "OK," I said as I wiped away tears and started walking. The hallway had just as little personality as the outside of the building. The walls were white, the floor was white, even the overhead fluorescent lighting provided a perfectly white light. "So Mark's down in the basement?" I asked.

"Well, that's complicated . . ."

Just then, a guy glued to his phone walked out of a door. There was no way to tell if he was playing *Go Wild*, so I dove through a wall just in case. "Do you think . . ." I looked around the room. "Whoaaaaa."

Inside the room I'd crashed were rows and rows of people watching computer monitors. Other workers wheeled around small projectors that displayed *Star Wars*–level holograms. Up front was a gigantic screen showing all sorts of numbers and moving charts. The whole thing looked like a NASA ground control room from the future.

"Is this where they make the video games?"

"That's not safe!" Mr. Gregory yelled. "You need to get out of there now and run to the basement."

"Definitely," I said, moving to the door at the other end of the room. "Let me just make sure that the guy's gone."

"It doesn't matter if he's gone or not," Mr. Gregory said, a little panicky. "You need to get out now!"

"OK, OK, I'm . . ." I stopped dead in my tracks. At that moment, I happened to glance at a computer screen and catch a familiar sight—the Statue of Liberty taking off like a rocket ship. "What is this?"

"Jesse! Out! Now!"

Two small figures jumped out of the crown. Two figures that looked just like me and Eric.

"Are they . . . are they watching us?" I asked.

"This isn't safe!"

I looked at another screen. It showed me and Eric blowing through a dark swamp on a hover tank. Another screen—Eric blasting me in the Rocky Mountains. Another—me flying through Hawaii with a jet pack. In fact, Eric and I seemed to be on dozens of screens around the room.

"Mr. Gregory, if they knew we were in the video game, why didn't they get us out?"

"Go to the basement!"

Was Mr. Gregory trying to hide something? I continued walking down the row of computers, every one displaying a video game. Some showed me and Eric playing *Full Blast*, while others seemed to just be regular Bionosoft video games—one was a racing game, another was a space shooter, another was a . . . Wait. I backed up to the space shooter. The main character had a weird expression on his face. Instead of the usual video game tough-guy look, this one had terrified eyes and seemed to be screaming. Also, he looked a little young. I scanned the room again. None of the video game characters looked happy to be there, and most seemed to be kids.

"What's going on?" I yelled. "Are they trapping kids in video games on purpose?!"

"If you don't get out of there now, I'm going to have to bring you in!"

Just then, a hologram at the front of the room flickered on. It showed an old man in raggedy clothes huddled into a ball. The man was shivering and rocking back and forth with his head bowed and legs pulled tight against his body. I edged closer to the hologram. There was something familiar about him.

At that moment, the old man looked up and turned toward me. I stiffened. Those eyes. Those bright-blue eyes. It was Mark.

CHAPTER 12

Mad Scientist

"MARK!" I screamed. "MARRRR—Oof!" Something tugged on my chest.

"I'm getting you out of there," Mr. Gregory said over my earpiece. I felt myself being pulled back across the room by the leash. I tried to fight it, clawing at everything around me, but it was no use—my hands just passed through everything I touched.

"Come on! Eric, what's going on?"

"He took my phone!" Eric yelled over the earpiece. "He took my phone, and he's reeling you back in!"

"You gotta help me—I think I found Mark!"

Suddenly, I heard a commotion over my earpiece. "Ouch! Hey!"

One second later, an out-of-breath Eric came on the earpiece. "I got the phone!" he yelled. "Get Mark!"

I ran to the front of the room screaming at the hologram of my friend. "Mark! Mark!" He never turned. When I reached him, I tried grabbing him by the shoulders. "We're going to get you out of here," I said. My hands passed right through his body. I climbed onto his hologram stand looking for something I could use to get him out.

"GASP!" I heard next to me. I ignored it. Maybe there was a portal in the base of the hologram stand.

"Do you see that?"

"Get it on the big screen and call security!"

The whole base of the stand seemed to be a projector. Maybe if I stuck my head through and looked around . . .

I suddenly became aware that the room had gone dead silent. I glanced up to find everyone in the room either locking eyes with me or staring at the screen up front. I turned around. The big screen now showed a live view of Mark's hologram, but it looked different than before. This time, a face stuck out of Mark's back—a face that looked just like mine.

"Uh-oh," I said.

"Uh-oh," the face on the screen said.

The room went nuts. All at once, people started screaming, jumping from their desks, and grabbing phones. Two security officers—one with a big beard and one with big muscles—ran at me while I climbed off the stand. I had to get out of there before somebody had time to turn on *Go Wild* and—

"Got him!"

Big Beard grabbed my foot. I yelped in surprise because I'd just gotten used to the idea of being invisible. The hologram seemed to interfere with *Go Wild* in an unfortunate way that temporarily turned me solid. I tried kicking. No good. I screamed. His grip tightened. In desperation, I yanked my foot as hard as I could, pulling him off balance into the hologram stand.

"OUCH!" he screamed as his eye hit the corner of the stand. He let go and grabbed his head.

"Sorry!" I yelled over my shoulder as I ran for the nearest wall.

Remain calm, a woman's voice said over a speaker in the room. *Activate Ghost Protocol.*

"WHAT IS GHOST PROTOCOL?!" I yelled as I dove through a wall. The emergency lights began flashing, turning the stark white hallway bloodred.

Remain calm. Activate Ghost Protocol.

I continued running across the hallway, through an office and into another hallway. Mr. Gregory came back on my earpiece. "You're the ghost," he said. "They won't stop until they find you now. This is what I was trying to warn you about."

"Wouldn't it have been easier to just tell me to stay away from holograms?" I yelled as I sprinted through a bathroom.

"It's more complicated than that."

We have a confirmed sighting of a digital ghost.

I crossed another hallway, ran through two more offices, and paused to catch my breath in an empty laboratory.

"This is a really bad place to stop!" Mr. Gregory said.

"Why do you keep telling me not to stop?" I asked. "What's going on?" I looked around the room. It was the type of lab you'd see in a mad scientist movie with bright-green goo in beakers, glowing electrical tubes, and a stretcher with straps for the arms and legs. The stretcher looked particularly scary.

"Jesse, you must . . ."

I threw the glasses across the room. Mr. Gregory was clearly hiding something, and I didn't need his voice in my head anymore.

Proceed with caution. This is not a drill.

"Squeak, squeak!"

I spun around to see a wall of cages full of squeaky, stinky rats. Well, actually only half the cages had rats. The other half had all been opened. Where were *those* rats?

If you encounter a ghost, report to a supervisor immediately.

I knew I should have started running again, but I couldn't stop looking through the lab. What could a video game company possibly need with a mad scientist laboratory? I turned my attention to the middle of the room where most of the electronics were. The main piece of equipment was a monstrosity of tangled wires, tubes, and metal reaching to the ceiling. On one side of the machine was a computer screen and on the other was what looked like a real-life video game ray gun.

Never interact with a digital ghost on your own.

I was about to examine the ray gun, but something on the screen caught my attention. I took a closer look. The screen was showing Sand Monster Island from *Full Blast*, but this time there was no golden-brown sand. Instead, the ground looked dark gray. And it was squirming.

At this time, please evacuate the building. Take all personal electronics with you.

Oh. Oh, gross. I'd found the other rats. A closer examination showed that the island itself wasn't moving—instead, it was covered with thousands of rodents all crawling over each other to find a way off the island. I turned and stumbled right into a desk.

QUADRANT FOUR CLEAR, a man's voice came over the speaker.

The desk was empty except for an open cardboard box in the center. Someone seemed to have cleared out in a hurry.

QUADRANTS TWO AND THREE ALSO CLEAR.

The cardboard box was filled with personal office knickknacks. There was a collectible *Full Blast* alien figurine, a few *Dilbert* cartoons, a picture frame. Wait. That picture inside the frame. I knew who it was.

LOCK DOWN QUADRANT ONE.

Smiling at me, with his hand on the electricity ball at the Science Center and his hair sticking straight up, was Charlie Gregory from my class. Next to the picture, I found a nameplate that removed all doubt as to the owner of the lab. There, engraved in cheap, gold-tinted metal, was the name "DR. ALISTAIR GREGORY."

Mr. Gregory was the mad scientist.

I dove for the glasses on the ground. "Eric, run!" I yelled into the earpiece. "Run from Mr. Gregory!"

"Get off of me!" Eric said. "Hey, stop . . ."

The earpiece filled with static. Then the lab door burst open.

CHAPTER 13

The Experiment

Four security officers wearing futuristic glasses stormed into the room. "THERE!" one of them shouted. They all ran right at me even though none of them had phones. Something about their glasses was letting them see me in the game. Instead of sticking around to find out how the glasses worked, I ducked my head under the floor and pulled my roll-under-the-bus move. This got me into the ceiling tiles of the level underneath, where I scrambled away from the lab as fast as I could.

"Perfect. Bring them here," a voice underneath me said.

I paused and peeked through a ceiling tile to see a large presentation room with tons of chairs facing a small stage and big screen. The room was empty except for a few security officers up front wearing the glasses from the future and a tall man with oily hair and a gross tan. He must have been important, because his portrait hung on the wall.

"I'll handle him," the man said to the security guards. Him who? I couldn't keep poking my head out of the ceiling like this without one of the guards seeing me, so I crawled left, shimmied down a couple of feet inside the wall, and slowly stuck out my head. It took a few seconds to line up everything perfectly, but when I did, I became virtually undetectable. That's because I'd managed to poke my eyes through the eyes in the painting like the bad guys in *Scooby-Doo*! All those years of watching cartoons had finally paid off. I didn't have much time to congratulate myself, because right then the prisoner marched through the door. I heard him before I saw him.

"This is a crime!" Eric yelled. "Unhand me!"

Unhand me? Where does he get this stuff? Four security guards marched Eric and Mr. Gregory to the front of the room. Eric struggled the whole way.

"I wasn't trespassing! I was playing in the woods! I want my lawyer!"

"No problem." The tan man held up his hand and pulled out his phone. "Who's your lawyer?"

Eric was taken off guard by the man's willingness to go along with his stupid demand. He stopped struggling and went with the first name he could think of. "Uh, Mulaney and Flynn?"

"Those injury lawyers with the cheesy commercials on daytime TV?"

"Mulaney and Flynn for the win."

"You don't have a lawyer, do you?"

"You don't know that!"

"Please," Greasy Hair said. "Have a seat."

Eric started to sit down and then tried bolting. A security officer pushed him into a chair.

"Thank you," the man said. "And welcome to Bionosoft! I'm Bionosoft founder and president Jevvrey Delfino."

"What have you done with Mark Whitman?!"

"Eric. That's your name, right? Eric?"

Eric refused to nod.

"Eric, I appreciate your concern for your friend. Loyalty is a trait that I hold quite dear." He gave a slight nod to Mr. Gregory. "Let me assure you that Mark is doing important work for myself and Alistair here."

"I don't believe you."

"Would you like to see him for yourself?" Jevvrey reached behind the podium and pulled out a ray gun that was identical to the one I'd seen in the lab.

"Jevvrey," Mr. Gregory whispered. "Please don't."

"Alistair, don't be so modest." Jevvrey turned to Eric. "This man is too humble to tell you, but he'll soon be known as the Edison of our time. Come, see the invention that will change the world." He held out the ray gun.

Eric, not being one to turn down an opportunity to check out a sci-fi ray gun (even if that opportunity came from an evil villain type), slowly made his way to the podium.

"That's it," Jevvrey said. "Here, take a closer look." He set the gun in Eric's hands. Eric carefully turned it over a few times, holding it as if the gun might decide to shoot a giant blast on its own at any moment.

"What you're holding in your hands is not only the future of video games, but the future of life on this planet. Imagine being able to travel anywhere . . ." He snapped. "In an instant. For example, where would you like to go right now?"

"Uh, home?"

Jevvrey laughed. "OK, besides that one. But what about Fiji? The Eiffel Tower? Antarctica? And not just places in the real world, but literally anywhere you can imagine. Atlantis. Gotham City. The Death Star!" Jevvrey started pacing back and forth on the stage and making large hand gestures as if he were giving a presentation. "With this technology, you can transport anyone to any place that you can build in a video game. It's better than virtual reality." He did a big, dramatic pause before delivering his final line. "It's the new reality!" Jevvrey stopped in the middle of the stage and smiled, waiting for Eric to cheer or something.

"Uhhhhhh, cool," Eric said in that voice he does when he doesn't really understand something.

Jevvrey pulled a canister of green gas from his pocket and took the gun from Eric. He spoke as he screwed the canister into the base of the gun. "This is plasma gas. Several months ago, Alistair discovered a method for using plasma to send living things into digital worlds. There's just one problem—the process costs millions. No matter how hard we tried, we couldn't make the gun affordable enough for people to buy. But," Jevvrey waggled his finger, "what if we didn't need a gun at all? What if we could use something that already has plasma in it? Something that's already inside every living room in America."

Eric was starting to get it now. "A TV?"

Jevvrey smiled. "I think you already know the answer to that."

"But why test it on us? We never agreed to be in your game!"

"I'd like to know that, too," Mr. Gregory said.

Jevvrey ignored him. "You agreed to test the game for Alistair, didn't you?"

"I didn't agree to be a human guinea pig! I almost got trapped for life!"

Jevvrey grinned and leaned closer. "Can you keep a secret?"

Eric backed away like Jevvrey had bad breath.

"You've actually gone inside *Full Blast* four different times."

Eric stared for a second, then shook his head.

"What's the matter? Don't remember?" Jevvrey walked back to the podium, picked up a remote, and turned on the giant screen behind him. Eric appeared on the screen, doing loops in a helicopter. "Remember this?"

Eric sat with a confused look on his face.

Jevvrey clicked a button, and the video changed to Eric snowboarding down a mountain while blasting aliens. "How about this?" Eric watched in silence as Jevvrey explained. "When you get out of a game the right way instead of breaking things like you did, your memory restores to the last save point. You can live years inside of a game without remembering a thing."

"But, but I did get out the right way! And I must have remembered, because I texted Jesse about it!"

"I know," Jevvrey said. "That was an unfortunate glitch that we've since fixed. And we've been able to fix countless more glitches just like it with the help of beta testers from around the world." He clicked the remote again, causing hundreds of boxes to pop up on the screen with all different types of people fighting through games. Some looked happy like Eric, but most looked downright terrified.

"So if Mark is one of your testers, why not just let him go?"

Jevvrey clicked the remote one more time. All the boxes disappeared except for one. It showed Mark, still huddled and shivering, looking worse than ever. "Through this whole thing, we've always had one question: What will happen when people die in these video games? Will they be gone for good, or do they come back here? If they come back, will they be ready to return to the video game again? Have we just discovered the fountain of eternal youth? According to our calculations, Mark's digital body is over 80 years old now." He turned to look at the screen. "He doesn't look well, does he? I think we'll get our answer any minute now."

Eric started looking around wildly. "Wait, why are you telling me all this?"

Jevvrey smiled. "I just want you to know what you're getting yourself into," he said as he aimed the plasma gun.

Eric tried to run, but the security guards pounced.

"Keep him still," Jevvrey said. "I don't want to waste this shot."

"ERIC!" I yelled as I jumped out of hiding. I ran toward Jevvrey screaming. "NOOOOOOOOO!" Jevvrey turned a few dials on the gun and aimed it at Eric. I dove in front of him.

ZIIIIIIING!

The plasma gun shot me square in the chest.

CHAPTER 14

Pirate!

I closed my eyes when the ray hit me. It felt all tingly, like I'd been blasted with a mouthwash hose or something. When the tingling stopped, I opened my eyes again, expecting to find myself in some dark video game dungeon. Nope. In fact, nothing actually seemed different. I was still in the Bionosoft conference room with Eric, Jevvrey, Mr. Gregory, and a bunch of guys wearing weird glasses. The only difference was everyone now seemed to be staring at me in disbelief.

"Jesse?" Eric said. "You're . . . you're back."

"That's the other one!" Jevvrey shouted.

One of the guards holding Eric lunged for me. Instead of running away like I normally would, I surprised even myself by rolling at his knees.

"OOF!"

I took him out and continued running toward Eric. The other guard holding on to Eric let go to lunge after me, too. When he let go, Eric tried to help me by pushing him over. Unfortunately, Eric wildly overestimated his ability to topple a 220-pound man and instead fell over himself. This turned out to be just the right move, because at that moment, another security guy came running at me from the other direction and tripped over Eric on the ground. As that guard fell, he grabbed wildly for anything he could reach, which just so happened to be the ankle of the last guard. In a matter of seconds, Eric and I had somehow taken out three bad guys.

"LET'S GO!"

I got two steps toward the door before a vice grip clamped onto my ankle. One of the security officers holding Mr. Gregory had abandoned him and was now dragging me to the ground. I kicked a couple of times, but he held on like his life depended on it. The bad guys were starting to get up. "Eric!" I yelled. "Keep running! I'll . . ."

"OWWWWW!"

The hand on my ankle loosened. I looked back to see Mr. Gregory's mouth clamped onto the security officer's other hand. One of the guards tore Mr. Gregory off of him, but not before I was able to kick myself free. "RUN!" Mr. Gregory yelled after me. "THERE'S STILL TIME TO RESCUE MARK!"

Eric and I scrambled out the door as Mr. Gregory did his best to keep the guards busy behind us. "Where to?!" Eric shouted at me like I had some sort of map to Mark. Instead of replying that I had no idea "where to," I led us through a random door. Inside, we found ourselves surrounded by green walls and tons of foam props. As we ran through the room, I grabbed a long pole, and Eric picked up a foam shield and curvy pirate sword.

I glanced over. "You planning on running into a foam pirate?"

"YOU NEVER KNOW!"

We reached the opposite side of the room just as a mob of security officers burst through the door we'd entered.

"Stop, or else . . ."

We didn't get to hear the rest, because we'd just run into our own "or else" as we rounded the corner into the hallway. It was the bearded security officer I'd yanked into the hologram base earlier. He now had medical gauze taped over his left eye. Between the big beard and patch, he looked exactly like a . . .

"PIRATE!" Eric shrieked.

The guy pulled out a Taser and shot it at Eric. Fortunately, Eric had a big foam shield to hide behind. As soon as the Taser prongs *THUNK*ed into the foam, Eric shrieked and—for reasons known only to him— spun in a screaming circle. That again turned out to be just the right move, since the spinning yanked the Taser out of the pirate's hand, swung it in a circle, and bonked him in the head, causing him to fall. Eric dropped the shield, and we ran down the hall to the stairwell.

As we approached the stairs, I noticed a security camera at the end of the hall. "How are we going to get anywhere with all these cameras?!"

Without breaking stride, Eric took my pole, aimed it at the security camera, and jabbed as we ran by.

FITZ!

"Problem solved!"

We took the stairs down two flights and *FITZ*ed two more cameras. We decided to open the door to an empty hallway, take out one more camera, and pick a room to hide in. The room we chose happened to be less of a room and more of a long, narrow junk closet.

"What is all this stuff?" Eric asked when we turned on the light. Old computers, bare circuit boards, and tangles of colorful wires overflowed from shelves onto the floor. Eric picked up half a robot while I looked around the room for some way to hide from the bad guys.

"There!" I shouted. The ceiling tiles at the end of the room had been moved to reveal a Jesse-size hole in the ceiling.

"And how are we supposed to get up there?" Eric asked. "Turn into Spider-Man?"

"With this!" I smiled as I held up my pole.

"I don't get it."

"Watch," I said as I backed up. I sized up the jump, counted to three, and started running toward the back wall with the confidence of someone who'd pole-vaulted in the Olympics and not just watched it on TV one boring Saturday afternoon. At the end of the room, I planted the pole into the back corner and jumped. If my foam pole had been too noodly, I would have flopped into the wall. If it had been to hard, I would have speared myself with it and fallen back to the ground. But since it was the perfect combination of foam and springy core, it vaulted me toward the open ceiling tile eight feet off the ground. As I flew through the air, I marveled at my good fortune. Who would have thought this would work! Maybe we'd escape after . . .

SNAP!

Just as I made my final push into the ceiling, the pole broke. I had enough momentum to roll into the ceiling, but my heart sank when I looked down to check out the damage. Eric stood there with two pieces of a broken pole in his hands.

"What now?" he asked.

Just then, we heard the security army storm into the hallway outside.

"THEY'RE ON THIS FLOOR!" someone shouted.

Eric started to panic. He looked around the room for something he could use to climb up to me, but it'd take an hour to build a tower of broken computers all the way to the ceiling.

BANG! BANG! BANG!

The security team had begun throwing open doors as they worked their way down the hall. Eric wedged his sword against the door between two shelves on either side of the room, buying himself a few extra seconds with his little barricade.

BANG! BANG! BANG!

Eric started throwing stuff everywhere as the bad guys got closer. I looked in the ceiling for some sort of rope or wire I could lower down to him.

BANG! BANG! BANG!

"Hey!" Eric whispered.

I looked down. He was holding a plasma gun. Or, more accurately, half a plasma gun. It looked unfinished, with wires sticking out of it and no touch screen on the back.

"Should I try to put myself in *Go Wild*?"

"No way!" I hissed. "You don't even know how that works!"

*BANG! BANG! **BANG!***

CLUNKCLUNKCLUNK!

The bad guys had found our room, and they were now trying to break through Eric's barricade.

Eric shook his head, grabbed a plasma canister from the shelf, and flipped a switch on the gun. It made a couple of *beep-boop* old computer sounds and came to life. He turned the dial on the back, screwed in the canister, and tossed me his phone.

"What's this for?!"

"To see if I make it."

CLUNKCLUNKCLUNK!

Eric pressed one more button, and the gun started glowing.

"Eric, wait!"

Eric didn't wait. He pointed the business end of the plasma gun at his chest, squeezed his eyes closed, and pulled the trigger.

CHAPTER 15

The Horde

"ERIC!"

I quickly brought up *Go Wild* on Eric's phone and scanned the room. Nothing.

"ERIC!"

Then, a flicker. A hand making a thumbs-up floated in the air where Eric used to be. Piece by piece, the rest of his body flickered onto the screen. "This is so cool!" he said as soon as he got a mouth. "I'm invisible, right? Oh man, I'm gonna capture so many . . ."

*CLUNKCLUNKCLUNK—**CRASH!***

The security squad burst through the door. I crawled back far away from the hole in the ceiling, and Eric rolled through the wall.

"I just rolled through a wall!" I heard Eric shout through the phone. "THIS IS THE BEST . . ." *Click.* I turned off the phone before any of the bad guys could hear it.

"Where did they go?" one of them asked.

"Look." I heard the sound of another one picking something metal off the ground. He got on the radio. "They ghosted. Lock it down and send in the horde." Then I heard a bunch of boots stomp off.

After a few seconds, I dared to quietly crawl back to the hole in the ceiling and peek into the room. It was empty. I took out the phone. "Eric? Eric?"

Without warning, Eric burst through the floor. "Ha ha! This is sooooo cool! I'm still trying to figure out my power, but look at this!" He stuck his head through the floor, then tried to do a handstand without hands. He wobbled a little, then fell over after a few seconds. He popped his head back out. "I'm still working on it, but . . ."

"ERIC!"

"What?"

"What's a horde?"

"How should I know?"

"Well, we should probably get out of here before we find out, right?"

"OK, yeah, whatever you want," Eric said distractedly as he karate kicked through the wall over and over.

Suddenly, one of the fur balls that had tried to eat my shoelace back on my porch appeared in the path of Eric's kick.

PUNT!

Eric booted it through the wall. Then another fur ball dropped from the ceiling onto Eric's head, and a third bit into his leg with a *CHOMP!*

"AHHH!"

A tower of five of them appeared right in front of his face, showed their fangs, and chattered angrily.

"THE HORDE!" Eric screamed as two more chomped onto his leg.

"What do we do?"

"UPGRADE ME!"

"How do I do that?"

"JUST FIGURE IT OUT!" Eric screamed as he wildly tore fur balls from his body.

I swiped and scrolled and finally found the upgrade menu. "Which one do you want me to do?"

"ALL OF THEM!"

I ran down the list, tapping every available upgrade. Five seconds and a hundred dollars of that guard's money later, I looked up. "Did I do it?"

Eric glowed like a purple fireball and grew before my eyes. His body got to twice its normal size, but his hands kept getting bigger and bigger until they reached the size of overstuffed beanbag chairs.

"YES! HULK SMASH!" Eric yelled in a slightly deeper voice than normal. He balled up his fists and started punching fur balls into next week. "WOO-HOO!" With his supersize fists of fury, Eric plowed through fur balls like a seventh-grader crashing the third-grade football game. But even as he joyously smashed balls of fur, I could see that he was outmatched. For every one fur ball that he squashed, three more would appear.

"Eric, there are too many!" He thumped the ground with his giant hands, causing a shockwave to ripple through the room and take out every fur ball in sight.

"See, I got it!" he said. But just during that four-word sentence, 10 new fur balls fell from the ceiling.

"I think they're multiplying!"

Eric continued punching and swatting and thumping, but I noticed he'd started glowing a little less brightly.

I looked down to see a meter on the screen nearing 25 percent.

"Give me a boost!" he yelled.

I found the "Boost Upgrade" button ($9.99) and clicked it. Eric glowed brighter and smashed harder, but the fur ball army had started multiplying so fast that even Eric realized that he needed a different strategy.

"Ouch! OUCH! Hey, I gotta get out of here!" he yelled as he started moving for the door.

"What about me?"

"Follow me so you can keep beaming me upgrades!"

"But I'm not invisible!"

Eric's body was completely covered in fur. "OUCH! Stop it!" *SMASH SMASH SMASH.* He ran into the hallway.

Well, I could either stay put and let my best friend get eaten alive by a horde of cute-but-deadly fur balls or follow along until I got Tased by a horde of angry security guards. I chose the Taser horde. "Wait up!" I yelled as I crawled through the ceiling.

When I got to the closet doorway, I removed a ceiling tile and looked down. Bingo. The door hung open, which meant I could roll through the ceiling hole, grab the top of the door, and swing myself down until my feet touched the doorknob, allowing me to make it to the ground without breaking an ankle. I put Eric's phone in my pocket, breathed once, twice, then rolled through the hole, missed the door completely, and totally broke my ankle on the ground.

"MMMRMMPH!" I said as I writhed in pain, trying to stay as quiet as possible in case any of my security guard friends had hung around. Fortunately, I found the hallway completely empty, allowing me to let out a little whimper as I hobbled to my feet. "Eric, this was the worst plan," I grumbled as I pulled his phone out of my pocket.

Uh-oh. The screen had cracked into a bazillion pieces. By the looks of it, I'd landed directly on it. I tapped the screen and got about a third of it to work, which was enough to find a long line of fur chasing Eric down the hall. I limped toward him on my almost-but-probably-not-totally broken ankle and pressed the upgrade button again.

WHOOSH! SMASH!

Eric punched the floor and wiped out the whole line in one shockwave. "Come on!" He waited for me to catch up until the fur balls started multiplying again.

If I wouldn't have been limping in a blind panic, I might have noticed something unusual—the horde kept appearing behind Eric, never in front of him.

We reached the stairs and started climbing. When we made it to the first floor, Eric started to run through the door. He immediately turned around. "KEEP GOING!"

I looked through the door's window with my phone. A sea of angry fur. Same thing on the next floor. It wasn't until the fourth floor up that we got a clear hallway. "This one!" Eric yelled.

"Hold on," I said as I powered him up again. He picked up the closest fur ball and used it as a bowling ball to knock down all the little monsters behind it.

"Don't you think it's weird that we haven't run into any security guys?" I asked. "They would have seen me on a camera by now, right?"

Eric shrugged. "Maybe nobody's watching the cameras because they're all chasing us." Just then, the ceiling rained fur balls. "Let's go!"

I put my head down and followed him again. Something didn't seem right about this whole thing. I didn't have time to figure it out, because almost as soon as we started running down the hallway, a wall of fur appeared in front of us.

"AHHH!" Eric screamed and ducked into the nearest door. I followed him into the dark room. As soon as I stepped into the room, I knew it was the wrong move.

SLAM!

The door behind us shut all by itself. For a few seconds, there was nothing but darkness and squeaking. Oh no. I knew that squeaking. Then the lights clicked on one by one, revealing rows of caged rats. We were back in Mr. Gregory's lab.

"Hello again, gentlemen."

Sitting in front of us with hands folded in his lap and a calm smile on his face was Jevvrey Delfino.

CHAPTER 16

Black Box

Eric immediately turned around and tried to run back out the door.

BONK!

He bounced off the door. He tried the wall. Same result.

"I'm sorry, but we've locked everything down," Jevvrey said.

Eric spun around. Jevvrey was looking at him through the futuristic glasses. He waved to Eric. "Bluetooth *Go Wild* goggles. $99.99. Available soon for preorder."

I looked around the room. Jevvrey had added a few things since I'd last seen it. For one, he was sitting on a swivel chair in front of a six-foot-tall black rectangle in the middle of the room. It looked like one of those supercomputers from the movies with switches and buttons and blinking lights all over it. The other thing was Mr. Gregory, sitting at his desk in front of a laptop, looking miserable.

"I was hoping you'd make it in time," Jevvrey said.

"In time for what?"

"We're about to find out what happens at the end of the game!" Jevvrey took out his phone and tapped on the screen.

"Mark?" Eric asked.

Jevvrey nodded. "He's fading fast now." He turned the phone around so we could see it.

Mark *was* fading. Not like his health or anything—he was actually disappearing from the screen. We could see right through him, and he was becoming more transparent by the second.

Jevvrey smiled. "Isn't this incredible?"

"Where is he?!" Eric yelled as he took a swing at Jevvrey. Of course, the punch went right through him because Eric was invisible. "WHERE IS HE?!"

Jevvrey laughed. "That's so cute that you still think you can rescue him. Isn't it cute, Alistair?" He turned to Mr. Gregory behind him. "Would you like to tell them Alistair, or should I?" Mr. Gregory avoided eye contact.

"Tell us what?" Eric asked.

"I'm sorry to be the one to tell you, but there was never anything you could have done to save him."

I'd had just about enough of Jevvrey. "You're lying!" I yelled. "Mr. Gregory said . . ."

"Mr. Gregory said what? Did he ever give you a specific plan for rescuing Mark?"

"Well, he . . ."

"Mark is in a Black Box," Jevvrey patted the machine behind him. "Black Boxes cost millions of dollars because they don't lose data. Nothing escapes a Black Box. But you already knew that."

I remembered Mark saying the exact same thing during *Full Blast*.

"Alistair didn't bring you here to rescue Mark. It's impossible to rescue Mark. He brought you here because I told him to."

Mr. Gregory continued looking away.

"Bionosoft was right on the edge of changing the world, and then you two escaped with our secret. We couldn't have that, could we? I told Alistair that if he didn't get you both into a Black Box, his son was going in instead. When he disappeared, I got a little worried that he was going to make a stupid decision, but then he showed up today with BOTH of you!" He turned to Mr. Gregory. "I never should have lost faith in you, Alistair."

I couldn't believe what I was hearing. I looked at Mr. Gregory for confirmation, but he wouldn't look back at me. He continued staring to the side like he had something to say but didn't want to say it. Jevvrey patted me on the shoulder. "I know it's a lot to take in. I'm so sorry. It's not your fault."

I kept my eyes on Mr. Gregory. It wasn't like he was avoiding eye contact—he was keeping his eyes on the exact same spot.

"Fire up the machine, Alistair."

What was he looking at? I followed his gaze across the room to the computer screen just behind Jevvrey's shoulder. The screen was showing the same thing I'd seen earlier—the rats on the deserted island. But they weren't clumped together in a tangled mass anymore.

Instead, they seemed to form groups that made shapes. I stared at the screen a few seconds longer until I saw it. Not shapes! Letters! Three rows of rats formed three distinct words.

R-E-A-C-H

I-N

E-R-I-C

DOWNLOADING
NEXT CHAPTER...
Data Rates May Apply

CHAPTER 17

Game Over

"Reach in Eric?" What does that even mean?

While Jevvrey screwed a plasma canister into a gun, I looked at Eric through my phone and got his attention. I motioned toward the screen with my head. He didn't understand. I motioned again, this time longer. He looked where I was pointing my head and nodded like he got it, even though he for sure still didn't get it.

"Look at the screen," I mouthed.

Eric squinted at me, squinted at the screen, squinted at me again, then suddenly whipped his head back at the screen. He stared at it for a while and then gave me a weird look. I shrugged and looked at Mr. Gregory. He glanced up from his computer and nodded ever so slightly.

"OK, I'm all set, Alistair," Jevvrey said after he'd finished connecting the plasma gun to the Black Box. "Start the software." He turned his attention to me.

"Anything you'd like us to tell your parents when you're gone?"

"I'd say, 'Just try it,'" I replied as I looked in Eric's direction while making a little reaching motion.

"Try it?" Jevvrey tilted his head. "Try to find you, you mean? Hmm. Wouldn't be my choice for last words, but who am I to judge?"

WHIRRRRRRRRR.

He fired up the plasma gun and pointed it at me.

"ERIC!" I yelled. "NOW!"

With nothing to lose, Eric ran for the computer screen. Jevvrey chuckled. "You're stuck in this room," he said. "So feel free to . . ."

He stopped midsentence when Eric reached his hand into the screen. Eric's hand didn't go through the screen like I'd expected—it actually went into the video game world. When Eric reached into the screen, a massive shadow fell over the tiny island.

"Whoaaaaaaaa!" Eric said.

"How are you doing that?" Jevvrey shouted as he adjusted his aim from me to Eric.

"Bring your hand down!" Mr. Gregory instructed.

As soon as Eric did, a giant hand appeared on screen. He brought his hand all the way down on top of the squirming mountain of rats. "GROSS!" He pulled his hand back out, which scooped about a thousand rodents from the island into the lab.

"What's going on?!" Jevvrey shouted while backing up.

Mr. Gregory did a little whistle through his teeth and pointed at Jevvrey. In one big clump, the rats all turned and ran at the Bionosoft president. "AHHHHH!" Jevvrey tried to run away, but he couldn't get two steps before the sandy rodents covered him from head to toe. He dropped the plasma gun as he tried to brush them off. "SO MUCH NIBBLING!"

As soon as Jevvrey dropped the gun, Mr. Gregory jumped from his desk and sprinted over. He scooped up the gun, aimed it at Jevvrey, and pulled the trigger.

ZIIIIIIING!

In an instant, Jevvrey and every last rat disappeared. A small screen on the Black Box flickered on and revealed Jevvrey running around in darkness with a mass of rodents chasing him. The whole thing was over in less than five seconds. I stood staring with my mouth open.

"To the basement," Mr. Gregory said as he ran back to the laptop on his desk. "We don't have much time."

"What just . . ." Eric was still standing by the computer screen, more baffled than ever. He tried to put his hand back into the video game but clunked it on the screen. He patted his body. "Am I . . ."

"Yes, you're back," Mr. Gregory said without looking up from his laptop.

"But, but how? I don't understand."

Mr. Gregory was typing furiously now. "Yesterday, I discovered that someone already inside of a video game can use screens as portals into other games. But—this is the important thing—the portals only work one way. So if you go halfway in and pull yourself back out, you break everything and come back to real life. In theory, it's the perfect way to rescue Mark."

"In theory?" I asked.

"Yes, in theory. Also in theory—by the way—holograms·act in a similar way, which is why I needed you out of that control room earlier."

"So you were never trying to put us into a Black Box?" Eric asked.

Mr. Gregory shook his head. "I had no idea Bionosoft was testing on innocent people without permission. Once I found out what had happened, I felt it was my responsibility to fix things. No matter what."

I looked down to see Jevvrey's phone at my feet. I picked it up and turned it on. Oh no. No, no, no. Please no. "Mr. Gregory?"

Mr. Gregory wasn't paying attention. "I'm just hacking security—there we go."

"Mr. Gregory?"

"Opening doors, disabling locks, shutting off cameras . . ."

"Mr. Gregory, I think you should see this."

"Now I'm going to have to put you two into *Go Wild* one more time, just long enough to get you safely to the basement . . ."

"Mr. Gregory!" I shouted with tears in my eyes.

He finally turned. I showed him the live video of Mark on Jevvrey's phone. It was totally black. "He's gone."

CHAPTER 18
For Real This Time

"We've got to get down there now," Mr. Gregory said.

Eric looked sad and confused. "But he's . . ."

"Maybe, maybe not," Mr. Gregory interrupted. He rummaged through the room until he found two more plasma guns. He dialed them in and then grabbed two armfuls of glowing green canisters. "Here," he said as he handed them to me and Eric. "If you see any security guards, blast them into a Black Box."

"So just like a real-life video game?" Eric asked, trying to hide his excitement.

"Except we can die for real this time," I chimed in.

Mr. Gregory threw his laptop bag over his shoulder and loaded his plasma gun. "Right, so be careful," he said as he opened the door and walked right into two security guards.

"Whoa!" one of them said while fumbling with his gun.

ZIIIIIIING!

Eric blasted him.

The other one went for his radio while ducking and rolling for cover.

ZIIIIIIING!

I missed.

"We need backup on Floor Four," he said. "The two . . ."

ZIIIIIIING!

Mr. Gregory zapped him. "Let's move!" he yelled.

We sprinted for the stairs at the far end of the hallway. "What do you guys think of maybe taking the elevator?" Eric asked, huffing and puffing as we neared the stairs. Mr. Gregory shook his head, reached for the stairwell doorknob, then changed his mind in a hurry when he looked through the window.

"I think that's a great idea," Mr. Gregory said, wedging a stop under the door. I peeked through the window myself to see five security guys running toward us. I raced across the hall and pressed the elevator button.

BAM! BAM!

The security guys put their weight into the door as the elevator arrived.

DING!

We piled in, pressed "B3" for the lowest basement level, and clicked the "door close" button over and over again.

CLICKCLICKCLICKCLICK.

The doors weren't closing. "WHY DO THEY PUT THESE BUTTONS IN ELEVATORS IF THEY DON'T WORK?!" I yelled.

*CLICKCLICKCLICKCLICK **BAM!***

The security guys broke through as the elevator doors started to close. One of them got a shot off.

CRACK!

The bullet hit the back of the elevator right between me and Eric. The doors finally shut before anyone else could fire. Our rest lasted for just a moment, though, because two floors down—

DING!

—the doors reopened to reveal two security guards with their weapons drawn.

ZIIIIIIING! ZIIIIIIING!

We zapped them straight to video game jail. The doors closed again, we went down one more floor and—

DING!

—went through the whole process again.

"Can you do something about this, Mr. Gregory?" I asked.

"Well," Mr. Gregory said as he pulled his laptop out of the bag, "there is one thing I can . . ."

DING!

This time, we all moved to the side of the elevator before the doors opened. Three security guys ran in without seeing all of us pressed up against the wall.

ZIIIIIIING!

Eric hit his guy.

ZIIIIIIING!

Mr. Gregory hit his guy.

ZIIIIIIING!

I missed my guy. Again.

"YOU!" he yelled. It was the big-bearded pirate guard from earlier. This time, in addition to his eye gauze patch, he also sported a bandage covering his whole head from the Taser incident. He'd apparently learned his lesson, because he was no longer messing around with a Taser. His gun was drawn.

CRACK!

With no time to reload his plasma gun, Mr. Gregory threw it at the guy's head. The gun hit him square in the face, causing him to stumble backward, whack his head against the elevator railing, and get knocked out cold.

"OK," Mr. Gregory pulled out his laptop as if nothing had happened. "Let's see what we can do about this elevator." After a few clicks, the elevator speaker made a chime sound. "That should do it," he said. Sure enough, we made it all the way to B3 without the doors opening again.

"Let's get Mark!" Eric yelled when we stopped moving.

"Wait," Mr. Gregory said. "Let me check one thing first." He typed on his laptop for a few seconds and sighed. He turned the screen around to show us. It was the B3 security camera, showing a hallway packed full of security officers. "They figured out where we were going."

"We can just zap them all, right?!" Eric asked.

Mr. Gregory looked at the three remaining plasma canisters. "Nope."

"Well, then we can sneak past them in *Go Wild*!"

Mr. Gregory pointed out security officers wearing *Go Wild* goggles. "Nope. Also, if they knew enough to send all this security, they knew enough to send a horde. We'd be toast in two seconds."

"Well, we can, uh, we can . . ." Eric tried to come up with something that would work.

"There's nothing we can do." Mr. Gregory slumped against the wall.

I looked around the elevator, which had become our own Black Box. Mr. Gregory buried his head in his hands. Eric tried to climb up to the elevator ceiling. Then there was the security guard pirate, who'd be waking up any minute now. I kept staring at the pirate. Wait. Maybe we did have a way out after all.

CHAPTER 19
Cook the CPU

Ten minutes later, the elevator doors opened, and we stepped onto floor B3.

"I don't think your plan's going to work," Eric whispered.

Back in the elevator, I'd remembered my time in Stu's phone. What if all three of us didn't have to sneak past the guards? What if we only had to get one person through the door? I explained my idea to Mr. Gregory and Eric. If Mr. Gregory captured me and Eric into his phone and took our pirate friend's clothes, he might be able to get us to Mark.

We got to work disguising Mr. Gregory. Once we put on the uniform, fitted him with the guard's *Go Wild* goggles, and covered his porcupine hair with the bandages, he could have been anyone. After we'd finished, Mr. Gregory took a deep breath and zapped the unconscious guard into a Black Box, then used his last two canisters to zap me and Eric into *Go Wild*. He immediately captured us into his phone, brushed himself off, and pressed the "door open" button.

DING!

Eric and I held our breath through the steady *CLUNK-CLUNK-CLUNK* of Mr. Gregory's feet on the ground. Finally, we stopped.

"No one is allowed in this room," a voice said.

"Is that so?" Mr. Gregory replied, trying to sound tough.

"It is."

Without missing a beat, Mr. Gregory responded with the most ridiculous paragraph of nonsense I'd ever heard. "If no one's allowed in, then who's going to cook the CPU? Who's going to parse the haptic system? Maybe you can tell me how the neural ADP array is supposed to generate all by itself!"

"Sir, I need you to . . ."

"ARE YOU GOING TO TRANSCODE THE DHCP MATRIX? ARE YOU?!"

"Listen," the security guard tried before getting interrupted again.

"Should I go back to Jevvrey P. Delfino—the man who signs your checks—and tell him that his server farm won't get indexed today because someone was playing Barney Fife in the basement? In fact, why don't you tell him yourself?" Mr. Gregory pulled his phone out of his pocket, causing me and Eric to fall over.

"What is he doing?!" Eric yelled.

We crouched in silence waiting for the security guard to make up his mind. "That won't be necessary," he finally grumbled. "Go ahead."

We heard the *WHOOSH* of a door open in front of us, the *HUM* of a million computers running at once, and, finally, the *CLICK* of a vault door sealing us in. When we were safely inside, Mr. Gregory teleported us out of the phone and onto the ground. "Whoa," I said once I got a chance to see where we were.

"Double whoa!" Eric said.

Eric and I found ourselves in the single biggest room either of us had ever seen. Giant Black Boxes like the one in Mr. Gregory's lab stretched past the horizon. Also the room had a horizon! Like an ocean! It was cold, too—a freezing fog covered the ground. "Where's Mark?" Eric asked, shivering.

Mr. Gregory didn't answer because he was on the phone. "115 Future Way," he said to someone. "They're holding children as hostages in the basement. Yes, I know it's a video game company. Just trust me!" He hung up. "The police are on their way."

"Wait, shouldn't we have started out by calling the police?!" Eric asked.

"We couldn't risk Bionosoft cutting the power to this room before we got here," Mr. Gregory said.

"OK, so where's Mark?" I asked. "Also, uh, you know he disappeared, right?"

Mr. Gregory pulled out his laptop and started walking. "We'll get to that when the time comes." We wandered in silence for the length of a football field before Mr. Gregory stopped in front of a big black tower that looked exactly like every other tower. "This is it," he said.

Mr. Gregory connected the tower to his laptop with a cord and started typing. Lights on the Black Box began blinking. A screen on the side of the tower powered up. "Check in there," Mr. Gregory motioned to the screen.

I walked over and put my head in the screen. "Mark?" I was greeted by blackness and silence.

Mr. Gregory typed a few things. "Try again."

"Mark? Can you hear me?!" I stuck my head in farther. "MARK!" My voice bounced around.

Mr. Gregory got back to work on the laptop. "I'm dialing back the computer's clock, but that can cause problems, so I'm trying to be careful." The Black Box started whirring louder.

I put my hand on the Black Box to lean farther into the screen but quickly pulled it away. The tower was burning hot.

"Hurry up!" Mr. Gregory shouted. "It's becoming unstable!"

"Mark! MARK!" My face got hot like I was leaning way too close to a bonfire. I couldn't give up, though. "MAAAAAARK!" I thought I saw something. Not a person or anything. Maybe just a pin of light. "MAAAARRGGRGRGRGRG!" My voice started garbling like I was talking through a bad Internet connection.

"Jesse! JESSSSsshhhhsss . . ." Mr. Gregory yelled something behind me, but he too was garbled and fading. The pin of light started growing into something—a finger? No, two fingers. Three fingers!

In a few seconds, a full hand appeared right in front of my face. A beautiful, wrinkly old hand. I reached for it.

That's when my whole body got sucked into the machine.

DOWNLOADING NEXT CHAPTER... Data Rates May Apply

CHAPTER 20

Chain Reaction

I tumbled through the darkness like I was skydiving, all while Mark's hand taunted me just inches from my face. Whenever I tried reaching for the hand, I just spun faster out of control. I panicked and screamed until—

SNAP!

I stopped, hanging upside down in midair. A hand had grabbed my foot—a hand attached to my best friend, Eric. At least I think it was Eric. His face looked really pixelated, and his mouth and nose kept switching places on his face. I turned back and grabbed for Mark's hand. It had started fading again. "GIVE ME A FEW MORE INCHES!" I tried to shout to Eric. Unfortunately, it came out as "GLBLRMF A FMWMFLSO NNCHZ!"

Eric either understood what I was trying to say or started losing his grip, because he let me slide down just far enough to reach Mark's hand. As soon as I touched it, I felt a rush of heat sweep through my body. I grabbed on with all my might.

"PPPLRLRPRLBGR!" I yelled. (That was supposed to be "Pull!")

We moved a couple inches. "PPLLRPGRL HRRRDGRR!" ("Pull harder!")

Eric's grip loosened again. At the same time, Mark's hand started fading faster. It slipped through my grip until I was only holding on to one of his fingers. Then, just a half second before I was going to lose my grip for good, I felt one final yank. I squeezed the finger harder than I've squeezed anything in my life as I tumbled out of the computer.

I landed on the ground with a *THUD* and opened my eyes. The Black Box towered above me, lights blinking and fans whirring like it was ready to launch into space. Mr. Gregory's face appeared. "Mark?" He whipped off his goggles. "Is that you?"

I sat up and looked next to me. There was Mark with all his fingers and toes and not looking one bit wrinkly.

"What . . . what happened?" he asked.

"You're back!" I shouted.

Mark looked around. The server room, with its giant black towers and scary fog, probably seemed more alien than the world he'd just come from. "Back where?" he asked as he got up. "Hey!" He bent his leg again. "My knee's not popping! Why isn't my knee popping?"

"That's cuz you're 12!" Eric shouted.

"What do you mean I'm 12?" Mark asked as he sat back down. "Are you telling me . . ." His voice trailed off, and he started to shake.

Mr. Gregory took a picture of Mark on his phone and turned it around to show him his own face. Mark stared at the picture for a few seconds, then touched his cheek. "I'm 12 years old," he whispered to himself. "I'm 12."

He stood up, flexed his foot a few times, then jumped in place. "I'm 12!" He ran around the Black Box, then leapt on Eric's back. "I'm 12, I'm 12, I'm 12!"

Eric promptly fell over because he is not great at piggyback rides.

"I can't believe you guys came back for me!" Mark said.

"It was all Mr. Gregory!" I said.

"Yeah, I was the Hulk and Jesse was Elsa, and there were all these fur balls, and you should see the plasma gun!" Eric shouted.

Mark smiled and nodded, even though he had no idea what even one word of that meant. Then a tear formed in his eye. "Are my parents still around?" he asked.

Mr. Gregory put his hand on Mark's shoulder and nodded. "Are you ready to go see them?"

Mark just hugged Mr. Gregory in response.

We heard a commotion in the hallway. "I think it's the police!" Eric yelled.

He led the way back to the vault door. "You ever playing another video game again?" I asked Mark as we walked.

"No way!" he shouted. "What about you guys?"

"Mobile games only," Eric said.

Mark gave him a weird look. "What's the difference?" Before Eric could answer, the Black Box interrupted with a high-pitched whine.

I turned around. "Mr. Gregory?"

The whine turned into a scream.

"Is it supposed to do that?"

All the lights started glowing bright red.

"It should be fine," Mr. Gregory said. "It's a little unstable, but as long as it doesn't . . ."

Mr. Gregory stopped midsentence when the box next to Mark's lit up red, too.

"Oh no."

"Oh no what?"

Mr. Gregory ran back to his laptop. The second box started screaming louder and louder until its screen lit up and something tumbled out of it. It was a kid.

We all stood with our mouths hanging open as the kid felt his body and face. "How old am I?" he asked. "How old am I?!"

We all looked at each other. At that moment, two more boxes lit up.

"Mr. Gregory, what's going on?"

Those two boxes started screaming.

"I think we just caused a chain reaction," he said without looking up from his computer.

Two more kids popped out of the screaming boxes, and four more boxes lit up.

"That's good, right?" Eric asked.

Eight new Black Boxes started screaming. The sound got so loud that I could feel a vibration in my chest.

Mr. Gregory looked up. His face was white. "Everything Bionosoft has ever written into a video game is coming out," he said.

Something started to appear out of the Black Box behind Mr. Gregory. Something big.

"Everything?" I asked. "What does that mean?"

ZAP!

The thing snapped into focus, giving me my answer. Suddenly, a few security guards and invisible fur balls felt like beginner mode. If we had trouble getting into Bionosoft, I couldn't begin to imagine how we'd survive long enough to make it back out.

Eric backed up. "Is that a . . ."

Yes. Yes, it was. There in front of us, as real as the ground under our feet, stood an eight-foot-tall praying mantis. The creature took a moment to look at all of us, then reared up on its back legs as seven of its friends appeared behind it.

"SCREEEEEEEEEEEEECH!"

About the Author

Dustin Brady

Dustin Brady lives in Cleveland, Ohio, with his wife, Deserae; dog, Nugget; and kids. He has spent a good chunk of his life getting crushed over and over in *Super Smash Bros.* by his brother Jesse and friend Eric. You can learn what he's working on next at dustinbradybooks.com and e-mail him at dustin@dustinbradybooks.com.

Jesse Brady

Jesse Brady is a professional illustrator and animator, who lives in Pensacola, Florida. His wife, April, is an awesome illustrator, too! When he was a kid, Jesse loved drawing pictures of his favorite video games, and he spent lots of time crushing his brother Dustin in *Super Smash Bros.* over and over again. You can see some of Jesse's best work at www.jessebradyart.com, and you can email him at jessebradyart@gmail.com.

MORE TO EXPLORE

If you want to create video games, you will have to learn how to write algorithms. Yikes! "Algorithm" sounds like a word that only scientists with lab coats and pointy mustaches should be allowed to say! Fortunately, algorithms are not that scary in real life. An algorithm is basically a set of instructions that tells a computer how to do something. If you can write a grocery list, you can write an algorithm.

The trick to writing a good algorithm is remembering that computers are stupid. Like super-duper stupid. Stooooooooopid. The mistake most beginner programmers make is assuming computers know things that haven't been explained to them yet.

A good algorithm for buying groceries wouldn't just list food that needs to be bought; it'd include everything from starting the car to driving directions, from the precise aisle location for every item on the list to the steps for paying at the register.

This section will teach you how algorithms work through two drawing lessons. In the first, you can test our algorithm for drawing an Upside Down Flamezoid. In the second, you're given the step-by-step drawings for creating a Fluffy Chupachu, but it'll be up to you to write down an algorithm for a friend to follow.

Upside Down Flamezoid

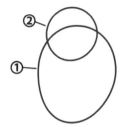

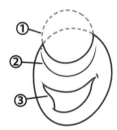

Step 1:

1. Draw a long oval to make the shape of the body.

2. Draw a small circle intersecting the top edge of the oval.

Step 2:

1. Erase the extra lines at the top of the body and circle to leave two pointy ears.

2. Draw an extra curve between the two points to add detail to the head.

3. Draw a shape for the mouth.

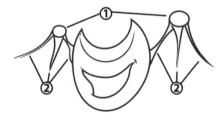

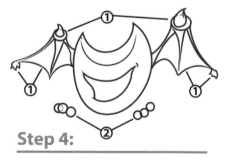

Step 3:

1. Draw two circles, one on each side of the body.

2. Get ready to finish the wings by drawing three thin lines connected to the circles.

Step 4:

1. Add detail to the wings by drawing horns, claws, and webs.

2. Add toes by drawing three circles on each side of the body.

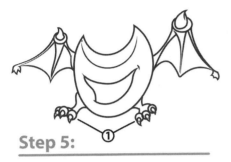

Step 5:

1. Finish the feet by adding legs and claws.

Step 6:

1. Draw sharp teeth inside the mouth.

2. Draw fur underneath the mouth.

Step 7:

1. Add fur to the outside of the body.

Step 8:

1. Erase any leftover lines to clean up your drawing.

Fluffy Chupachu

Now it's your turn to write an algorithm!

Steps:

1. Take a few minutes to write instructions for the steps below. Be as clear and specific as possible.

2. Give only your written instructions to a friend. Don't let him see these pictures!

3. Tell your friend to draw his best Fluffy Chupachu using only your written instructions.

4. Test your algorithm by comparing his finished product to ours. Was it close? What would you do differently next time?

Step 1:

1. _____

_____

_____

2. _____

_____

_____

Step 2:

1. _____

_____

_____

2. _____

_____

_____

Step 3:

1. _____
_____
_____

Step 4:

1. _____
_____
_____

2. _____
_____
_____

Step 5:

1. _____
_____
_____

Look for these books!

DUSTIN BRADY

CUBE KID

DOUG SAVAGE

Will Henry

by LINCOLN PEIRCE
New York Times Best-Selling Author

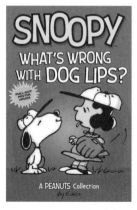

A PEANUTS Collection